To Mom and Sophie.

The lady who made it all possible

And the girl who can do the impossible.

Thank you for always believing in me.

This is a work of fiction. The characters are fictional. The places are real, for the most part, but some were changed to further the story. The events are fictional. Any resemblance to anyone living or dead is completely coincidental.

And no, using the stuff in this book for "magical spells" is not a good idea, so don't do it.

Other books by this author:

<u>The Statford Chronicles</u>

Volume I: The Sincerest Form of Flattery

Volume II: In The Details

Volume III: The Blame Game

That You Do So Well

By John G. Walker

Dedication and Acknowledgements

You folks know what? I almost didn't make it.

Thanks to the vagaries and the slings and arrow of outrageous fortune, I almost didn't get this book written. It sat at about 33000 words in November, just after I finished my National Novel Writing Month project, and it was terrible. I mean, it was worse than terrible.

It was boring.

That, my friends, is a cardinal sin when it comes to any book. If your readers would rather do their taxes than read your work, it's a problem. So, thanks to my editor, I scrapped it all save for about 1500 words. I was inconsolable for days. I was afraid that I had lost the way into the world of the Statford Chronicles, and after only three books. There's almost nothing worse for a writer than having pretty nifty characters with nothing important to say or do. It's like a Ferrari (or a Chevy Tracker) with no gas. Fun to look at, but pretty much nothing more than a really heavy paperweight.

So it was with a blank screen and a flashing cursor that I tentatively wrote the words "Chapter One" for the second time for the same book. I decided to take a new tack with the whole thing, and I think it turned out pretty well. This will make the fourth volume of the Chronicles, and I really feel like I can connect to it a lot better now that I've gotten this one down.

As such, without further ado, the following deserve thanks, blame, or both for being influences in my life and my writing.

My mom, who is of course just completely wonderful for listening to me ramble on and on about voodoo and liquefied people and not calling the men in white coats on me. Love you.

My niece Sophie, the self-rescuing princess, and the one who keeps me believing in the impossible. You have been, are, and always shall be awesome.

My sister for dealing with having a brother like me. Seriously. We geeks can be rather a tough burden to deal with. I know it's a chore for her, and she handles it fantastically.

My gramma for keeping me on my toes, and always making me smile. Thanks, Chief!

My editor Erika Pryor for dealing with me and making all these words come out in the right order.

Starla Huchton, the complete genius who makes the covers I keep having to write books worth of putting between them. An amazing artist, and an awesome author. Thank you.

A clear ton of people I listened to, read, and am completely in awe of on a daily basis. Dave Robison, Paul Cooley, Veronica Giguere, Cedric Johnson, Martin Spernau, and everyone in the RoTaNoWriMo group on Facebook. Thank you all for not only accepting my insanity, but saying that it was expected.

For Monty, who always had a good word for me when I went in to GameStop, and always treated everyone with respect and kindness. He passed away during the writing of this tome, and he is missed.

To all of my faithful readers. What can I say? I thank you for staying with me this long, and I hope you'll stick around. There are a few changes going on, and you don't want to miss a thing.

So sit back, relax, and let's see what happens. Again, my thanks to you all.

-jw

Chapter One

If I thought this plan was going to go easy, the random and incessant pounding on the doors showed what the world thought of my wishes.

"Susana!" I moved to the center of the nearly-empty room, trying to see in all directions at once. "Cover the south windows!"

The light of my life shouted back at me, completely worn and exasperated, "Which side is the south?" There was blood splattered on her hands and clothing, thankfully very little of it her own.

I pulled the mental map of the area up in my head, trying to remember which side of the room the sun rose on. That involved me remembering the patches of hell on earth we had gone through to get to this farmhouse out of Little House On The Prairie. It was a simple house with two floors, no separating walls and wide-open space where I could see everything, whether I liked it or not. From the style and the disrepair, I figured it had to be a half-century old. The walls were sturdy, most likely brick, though there were too many damned windows for me to have any sort of feelings of security. Frigging southerners and their desire for a breeze of the godsdamned veranda.

All that architectural crap aside, I recalled that the road we had taken had been roughly east-to-west. Taking a semi-wild guess, I pointed at the windows to my left. "That one. Make sure none of the bastards get in here."

She did as I asked, her long black hair coiled tight in a braid. Susana Magdalena Iglesias y Marquez was not used to taking orders, rather giving them, especially from her husband-to-be. The shotgun across her back had spat its last load of pellets into one of the things that was throwing itself at the barricade, and I knew the pistol she carried had two bullets remaining. Muck covered what blood did not, streaking her face like septic war paint; her clothes were tattered, more a memory than material, the tawny flesh showing through the rents and the tears in the fabric. Blood welled up in streaks where she had been clawed. She had a black eye from a club-like arm striking her, but withstood the pain like a champ. It hurt my heart to see the marks, though.

As for me, I knew I wasn't looking much better. In point of fact, I likely looked the worse for wear. My usual form of dress, jeans and t-shirt, were torn from being grabbed by scrabbling claws, and my Chuck Taylors were squishing with mud and swamp. The back of my head throbbed from when some son of a bitch had clocked me with an ax-handle, and I couldn't tell if it was bleeding anymore. I had learned the hard way that head wounds bled until they were damned good and ready to stop, and my dark brown hair still had a sticky, matted feel to it. My body ached from the exertions I had been doing; even though I had been working out more at the gym, I still had a touch of a gut. My arms and legs burned from running through muck and hammering nails into boards that barely stretched across the windows. I wasn't used to this much work while operating in a high state of terror that I was doing my best to shove down into the bowels of my mind until I had Susana and my mom out of harm's way.

I was spinning my wheels at the moment, trying to think of some way out of this mess. The pounding on the doors and windows was terrible, random banging and bashing. Boards nailed over the windows shuddered with each blow, and they would not last long. I saw one of the boards on one of the eastern windows splinter. Aiming between the slats, I fired the revolver in my left hand, my brain ticking off the first of the last six bullets that gun would ever fire. If things didn't get any better, I likely wouldn't see the light of morning.

The roar of the gun snapped me out of my fog, focusing me back to the present. I knew the bullet had found its mark; missing was not something I did often. I also knew that it had just been a waste. There were a few dozen out there, and more showing up as time went on. The only thing slowing them down was the mud and the swamp, and even that wouldn't pose enough of a problem to buy us a respite of any use.

We had been on the run for way too long. Literally on the run, as our SUV had thrown a rod through the block on some backwoods road a score of miles from civilization. The car was a burnt carcass in the middle of a dirt path a couple of miles from where we had made our escape, the flames a desperate gamble for desperate people. It hadn't made a damn bit of difference. We could have dropped napalm on the countryside and followed up with a nuke and they still would have found us.

They had our scent.

"We can't hold much longer." My mom's voice was calmer than any sane person's would or should be in a similar situation. Like Susana, she had her hair pulled back into a sensible tail, though hers was a reddish-blonde shot with a lighter blonde. Aveline Statford kept in amazing shape, even though she was almost at her third time hitting twenty years old. Most people half her age wished they were in as good a condition. Though her body was trained to razor-sharpness, her mind was even sharper, making her likely one of the deadliest people on the face of the earth. Mom's light eyes caught every detail, missed nothing, saw everything. She thrust a wrought iron poker through the barrier at the window, her position at the north side of the room as precarious as Susana's and mine. There was a terrible crunching sound before she pulled the metal back into our refuge. She thrust it forward again only to have it ripped from her grasp. I heard her bite back a hiss of pain and anger at losing her weapon. "This is getting bad."

"That's an understatement, Ma." Ever since I had been old enough to figure out the trips she went on weren't vacations but missions for the government, my mom had been the rock at the center of the universe; unbreakable, unshakable, unstoppable. There were members of Congress who checked with her on what to wear, let alone what to think. She had negotiated deals upon which the world powers had listened to her words, and she never cracked.

Now, though... She sounded scared.

Not that I blamed her. I was in a low grade of panic myself, and that only because I was likely riding high on endorphins. What was banging and bashing against the wood and stone of the shelter we had found was the stuff of nightmares. They could be destroyed; that the three of us had proven repeatedly over the last several hours and miles. Bullets worked, as did blunt force trauma. Susana had even used a machete for the job. Rendering these things inert wasn't the problem; the problem was there were too godsdamned many of them.

"We're running out of options." The words were out of my mouth before I could stop them. I threw a knife at the questing hand that had broken through the hastily-nailed boards over the long-gone windows. The blade sunk into near the hilt, trapping the hand on the windowsill. As I watched, the blade cut through the flesh, spilling a mixture of dust and a sickly glossy fluid from the wound. The owner of the hand pulled and the knife stayed embedded in the wood of the sill, slicing jaggedly through bone and sinew. My little act of defiance had done exactly squat to stop the swarm, and had deprived me of a pretty decent knife.

My eyes went to the staircase along one side of the wall. It was old, wooden, rickety, and looked to be about as sturdy as the economy built on mud. For what I had in mind, it was perfect, at least for the moment.

"Fuck it. Get up the stairs!" I shouted. It wasn't much of a plan or a shelter; in fact, it wasn't likely to buy more than a couple of hours, but it was better than nothing. The first of the windows burst in, with hands and arms poking through, questing for whatever they could grab. I pushed my mom and my fiancée up the stairs, trying to get them to move faster. Mom had thrown down several of those chemical glowsticks. We could see, but the light played hellish shadows across the walls.

I snarled as one of the things pushed itself through the hole in the glass. This was totally not in the job description.

Oh, right; it might be helpful to introduce myself at this point. Thomas Statford, private investigator and Keeper of the Conclave. Most of the time, my clients were of the normal variety, whether it be cheating husband or wife, insurance scam, or missing relative. Those are the kinds of cases I enjoy. They're simple, direct and to the point. You see, I can reason with some guy pissed-off that his wife is getting schtupped on the side, even if he's swinging a gun around threatening to put a bullet in my head; that's a piece of cake and, while I've been both shot and shot at many times before, it's something I can understand. Bullets are nice and normal. They hurt like hell, but they're normal.

When I have to don the hat of Keeper, though, is when things get messy. The Conclave is for all intents and purposes every god, goddess, demon, and celestial power that exists, and they have their own government of sorts. Think of it like the United Nations for deities, and it's just as dysfunctional as it sounds. All of the gods exist, forming the Conclave to keep one or more deities from turning reality into Silly Putty. Don't think it impossible; anyone who has ever met Eris, the Greek goddess of Chaos, would say she'd do it just for kicks.

They did decide to have a mortal representative, completely neutral, granted the power to mediate any disputes between the gods as needed. That sounds niftier and more powerful than it actually is. As the Keeper, my designation was like a hall monitor, though I did get a few perks. I kept the gods from affecting the mortal world any more than necessary. This included averting the occasional kidnapping for procreation and pleasure, floods to stop seaside developments, the raining down of fire and destruction of a torqued-off god of war when his football team chokes at the Super Bowl, and various other little things that could end life and the universe as humanity knows it. On the other side, I also kept mortals from sticking their noses (and other extremities; don't ask) into the business of the gods. That meant stopping sacrifices to whatever deities some chowderheads decided to worship, vandalism of shrines, activations of places of power that would allow one of the Elder Gods to come forth and wreak havoc upon an unsuspecting world, and just general nuisances that made my life interesting and painful. For doing this great and important task, I would get the following: my ass kicked on a monthly basis, possible death and dismemberment on a daily basis, immunity from the gods themselves but no protection from their minions, and the knowledge that the world will keep on trucking through this universe in more or less the same shape if I survived the beatings and shootings and burnings.

Okay, so what I do would be a dream job for a masochist of celestial proportions. Unfortunately, no one gets interviewed for it; you just get it, like a club foot or red hair or freckles. You just have it, whether you liked it or not. What you do with it is up to you. I decided to be a detective. My mom wanted me to be in government work, and my sister wishes I had been an interior decorator, even though I kept her on retainer and in business. I like to help people, and I do that by bringing matters to a close, one way or the other. Sometimes things end well, like when I helped a child back to his family safe and sound. It gives me a warm fuzzy feeling inside when things end well for everyone concerned.

Sometimes, though... sometimes they end in blood and tears.

This was starting to look like one of those times.

The staircase was as shaky as an epileptic in an earthquake. Once Mom and Susana were safe behind me on the second floor, I took the crowbar I had put up there earlier and began bashing the steps. Splinters flew with every strike, and I started to feel a little better, a little more secure. I knew I had at least a minute before I had to worry about being attacked.

The nearest five steps were gone, broken beyond recovery. I took a breath as I pulled myself completely away from the entrance to this second floor. The upper floor was almost a mirror image of the first, though the low roof peaked in the middle, giving a little bit more head room. It was more a bedroom than anything else, as evidenced by a bed, a vanity, and some drawers. There was a small bathroom on the western wall, which was out of place considering the almost studio-like construction of the building. I was past the point of caring, though; this room was someplace we could relax and possibly regain our strength for us to do what needed to be done before it was too late.

Hell, for all I knew, it was too late.

"You truly are in deep this time, Thomas." The new voice cut through my fatigue, bringing a weary smile to my face. It was a mellow sound, clipped and cultured.

My eyes had slipped shut for a moment. I had sat down away from my mom and Susana, who were taking a quick inventory of our supplies. It was quick because we didn't have many to begin with. "I noticed, Larry." With the hand not holding the crowbar, I scratched the back of my head before leaning against the wall. The pain was down to a dull roar, the flow of blood a trickle. Below me, I heard them milling around, reaching for the dim light above. "About time you showed up."

Larry, or Larrisimus, as he's more properly known, tutted at me. "I tried to warn you, Thomas. This was not the best idea you have ever had. You are trapped."

"How long until sunup?" My head pounded when he told me. "That long? We can't last that long. Hell, we're lucky we made it here."

"It is worse than that, and you know it." I opened my eyes on my partner. Larry gazed back evenly, his faded blue eyes looking out of an unlined but careworn face framed by wavy blonde hair. He was wearing some amazingly stylish suit the color of vanilla, which I would have found ridiculous had the owner of the suit not been a spirit. Larry was pretty much a source of information about every god, goddess, demon, deity, wise man, mythological creature and Thing That Should Not Be But Is, having existed through the centuries, working with one Keeper after another since time immemorial. In a world where I damned near stood alone against the forces of whatever wanted to destroy the world or at least remake it in some twisted image of insanity, Larry was with me, imparting advice, tactics and commentary against whatever I faced. We had been through a lot together, and I had learned I could count on him. He was intangible, inaudible to everyone except me, and possibly my best friend.

Of course, that didn't mean he couldn't be a pain in the ass.

"There are hundreds of them milling around, Thomas." Larry sounded genuinely worried. "They definitely have your scent."

I rolled my eyes. "Oh, you think? I couldn't tell."

Larry raised an eyebrow at my sarcasm. "Such a tone will not help you, nor will staying here. Eventually, they will get up here, and they will have you."

"Any good news?" Mom and Susana looked at me like I was only half-crazy; they were used to my having conversations with things only I could see.

"Some. What you are looking for is two miles north-by-northeast." Larry looked at me with obvious trepidation on his face.

"That's the good news. What bad news aren't you telling me?"

He took a deep breath, which was almost surreal considering he didn't need the air. "You have only thirty minutes left to stop it."

I cursed under my breath and came to my feet, checking the loads again on the revolver. Five bullets left, which left me about a bazillion shots short of being able to make it through the mass below me. "We really need to work on your delivery, Larry."

"What's wrong?" Susana looked concerned at me as she nursed a couple of bruises from our flight from the car.

"The usual good news and bad news." I started looking around for more supplies as I relayed what Larry told me.

"He does need to work on his bedside manner." Mom's voice was dry as she wrapped another makeshift bandage around Susana's forearm. "What's the play?"

I laughed, the first laugh I had had in what seemed like forever. It was a rusty sound, filled with resignation against what I had to do. "I was hoping you had one, Ma." I put the gun in my waistband at the small of my back. "If you don't, I've only got one choice." Tearing the sheets off the bed, I sat down and wrapped the cloth around my arms, the better to protect from bites and claws and whatever else might happen. My mom came over and helped, as did Susana. In my right pants pocket, I felt the gift I had been given pulse in time to my heartbeat. I had no idea how or why I still had it, but I figured I'd need it eventually.

That's what the old crazy lady had said, anyway.

"You don't have to do this, Tommy." Susana's eyes were filling with tears, both in anger and sadness. "There has to be another way."

I shook my head and gripped the crowbar tightly in my right hand. My arms looked like something from the set of a movie about mummies, though I bet the pharaohs never had worries like I did. "We're under half an hour, babe. I can do two miles in the dark in that time. I'll draw them off so you and Mom can get out. If it goes bad, you two will be out of range, and Ma," I looked at the lady, "you can use the TWERP method."

Mom smiled sadly. "I hate when you call it that."

"Regardless, it is what it is. If all goes well---"

"*When*," both women interrupted.

"If all goes well, I'll likely need pickup. Don't leave me hanging."

Susana helped me to my feet, strength still in her. "You better come back to me."

My smile came automatically. "Hey, look what it's taking to get me away from you." I looked to my mother, tears rolling down her cheeks. "Look after her until I get back, eh?" She didn't trust herself with words, just pressing a small device in my hand. I looked at it and whistled. "Where the hell did you get this? Gods, where the hell did you hide it?"

Mom inhaled deeply, bravado trumping emotion for the moment. "Just make sure you use it well."

I pulled Mom into a hug, knowing full well it might be the last time I did so. "Take care of her, Ma," I whispered. "She's everything."

"You do that yourself, Tommy." She squeezed me hard, strength in her embrace. "You better."

I released my mother and turned to Susana. We held hands a moment before I moved closer to her. She pulled away. I was a bit puzzled by her reaction.

"No, *gringo*. None of that 'little woman sends her man to war' shit." The words were costing her, I could tell. "You come back to me in one piece. You show me that I'm worth coming back to." She took off the ring I had put on her finger when I asked her to marry me and slipped it on my left pinky. "And you damned sure better bring that back."

This time, I was the one who couldn't trust my voice. I nodded and kissed the palm of her hand. Even with the mud and muck on her, I could still get her scent. I let it fill my head with strength before I kissed her palm again and released her. Walking away was the toughest thing I had ever done in life, but I did it, heart heavy but with purpose.

I pushed the window up, rust squalling against metal. That noise brought a fresh cacophony from below and without, grating on my ears and my mind worse than the window could ever cause. I stepped through the window and onto the roof, trying to gauge the right place to jump off. All around, I could see more forms approaching the solitary house, lurching and slumped.

"Larry, which way?" I forced down my fear and anger and pain, an almost-impossible task.

The spirit pointed to my right, and I wasn't sure how I couldn't have seen the eldritch glow before as it burned through the night, even from that distance. Though it was only a pinprick of light, against the dark it was almost impossible to miss. I knew I would have no trouble knowing which way to go. It was just a matter of getting there.

"I could use a distraction," I said to the women inside.

They obliged instantly, going to the window opposite me and shouting, screaming and caterwauling for all they were worth. They bashed together metal and wood, the pounding a clear rhythm in the dark. I heard the noises below me grow louder, then subside as they went to the other side of the house, arms reaching up, questing for two of the most important women in my life. They were being bait for me to make a run for it. Even if I was making a run to stop this insanity, I was still running. I hated myself for it, even though all three of us knew it was necessary. So, with a heavy heart and a snarl against the forces of whatever the hell was out there, I leaped into the night. My jump was flawless.

My landing, however, left something to be desired.

Chapter Two

Wait a minute. Let me start from the beginning.

Susana and I had by necessity and my own boneheadedness planned our wedding together, something most couples do when they're stupid in love and want to spend their lives together. It's archaic, it's silly, and I had no doubt in my mind that she was the one for me. Cue the sappy music if you want; she had been with me through thick and thin. From being kidnapped by a psychotic Russian trying to become a god, to helping clear the name of the fallen archangel, thereby averting Armageddon, to stopping a fifty-mile-wide firestorm caused by an irate Chinese fire god, Susana had been at my side. She rarely questioned, but never faltered and never wavered. You don't find love like that often in this world, and when you do, you hold on to it and treasure it.

You also don't do what I did and forget to set up the damned ceremony and honeymoon. If you're looking to piss off the love of your life, that's a great way to start. It's kind of like shooting the Pope to get on the express elevator to Hell; it's hard to find a faster way to screw up.

Give me half an hour and I can plan to survive anything. It's one of the traits I share with my hero, the Batman. That guy can be locked in a room orbiting a far distant sun, without his utility belt, wearing just his skin, having only his toothbrush and he still makes Superman's feet sweat in fear. He's my idol; nothing gets him down, nothing makes him worried and he always has a plan. Always.

 Of course, the Dark Knight never had to get married. If he did, I must have missed that issue.

 That was where I found myself on that fine autumn day: planning and planning. I had kind of misled the love of my life before when I said I had everything for the wedding and honeymoon set up. What I really had done was make an appointment to set everything up. Apparently, there is a huge difference in the two, and as a guy I didn't see the difference. I was about to be schooled.

 Right then I was on semi-vacation from the weirdness, though if I wasn't careful, blood and tears were going to flow, namely mine. Susana was with me on this trip to the travel agent, which I felt was a good idea, since the last thing anyone should do is plan something this big without their spouse involved, be they future or current. It was an unseasonably warm mid-autumn afternoon, and Susana was dressed down, a pair of jeans, a sweatshirt for her alma mater, and leather boots. Her dark hair was pulled back into a simple ponytail, two bits of hair framing her face. Though beautiful and a total girl when it came to bugs, she was one of the toughest cops I had ever met, an amazing woman, a wonderful friend, and I had no idea how I had gotten her in my life, let alone agree to marry me. I wasn't going to complain, though, not one bit. Susana was one of the most amazing people I knew, and that she put up with me and the weirdness was either a sign of her love or plain insanity. Maybe both; who was I to judge? After all, I talked to invisible men and gods.

"Are you kidding me?" Susana Magdalena Iglesias y Marquez said as we walked to the travel agency. "You don't have the tickets yet?"

"It's not like we don't have time," I said, knowing my words were likely falling on deaf ears. "We've got, what, five months?"

"Maybe," she said. "We don't even know where we're getting married, do we?"

"Well," I stammered, "it would depend on where we're going." Susana rolled her eyes at this. "What?"

"*Men.*" Her tone was of pure disgust, and that one word was an entire denunciation of the male gender. "Don't you know what goes into getting married?"

I shrugged. "Be gentle. It's my first time."

Susana did a double-take, and then laughed. "Damned well better be the last time," she said. "Come on, *gringo*. Let's get this started."

We walked into the travel agency, out of the cold and into the not-so-cold. The place, called Fly By Day, was pretty deserted, which didn't bode well. There were the stock "See Exotic Des Moines!"

posters on the wall, with different places inserted for Des Moines along with different locales, and a couple of desks. It was like something out of a movie or cheesy TV sitcom about travel agencies. Only one desk was occupied this Saturday, which kind of surprised me. I figured most folks would want to plan out vacations on a weekend. Of course, what I knew about being a travel agent could be written on a grain of rice with room to spare. The agent at the desk was a matronly woman, at least in her late fifties, with a throwback hairstyle of yesteryear. The blonde frizz should have been out of place, but it seemed to work for her. Her glasses, held hostage by a chain, were perched on her nose as she looked over them while we came in. She was talking on the phone as we looked around, being very animated with both voice and hand gestures. A distracted smile formed on her face when she saw us, and we waved to her in unison. The lady raised a hand in return, waving us over. She was one of those kinds of people who thrive in constant pressure: perpetually looking frazzled, yet completely in control. The lady was the epitome of chaos under glass.

Susana and I took seats in the chairs she indicated while she finished up the call. I was rather in awe of the lady's voice, commanding yet kind, chiding but sweet. It was like listening to my mom on the phone when someone wasn't doing what she thought they should, which was often. It was that tone that said you can do what you want to do, but it won't end well, so do it my way, and you'll see that it works. Everyone's heard that voice, and it seemed to be working.

"I promise you, this will be the best trip you've ever taken," she said smiling. The nameplate on the desk read Aletha Dallas, the nameplate itself nearly obscured by the papers and other debris that seem to collect on any flat surface in any office. "You will absolutely adore Bermuda. It's one of those perennial vacation spots that are once-in-a-lifetime trips!" She listened for a moment, then, "No, there haven't been any of those silly bad things happening there in quite a while. The authorities there have clamped down quite a bit, and it's mostly just those ridiculous young people." The lady made a non-committal noise and then said, "I know, but you're much too mature for such goings-on. Clubs? Bars? Where I have you going is a beach, with sand, surf, some light music playing. Nothing like what goes on at the other side of the island. Bermuda is completely for you!"

There were a few more minutes of back and forth, but it seemed that Ms. Dallas got her way. When she put the phone down, there were a few seconds of silence, broken only by her humming as she wrote down a few notes. "So how can Aletha Dallas, travel agent extraordinaire, help you, Mister and Mrs...?"

"Tom Statford," I said. "This is Susana Marquez."

"Oh, I'm sorry. I thought the two of you were together." She seemed embarrassed.

"Well," I said, smiling, "we are getting married. That counts as together, right?"

Aletha's face lit up with sheer sincere pleasure. "Congratulations! I take it you're the bride?" she said to Susana.

"No, I'm his mistress. He's just terrible at picking things out for women," Susana replied straight-faced.

I smothered a laugh. "Yes, she's my fiancée, and she's been a bit stressed," I said. "You see, we're getting married next year and we want---"

"A wedding abroad!" Aletha squealed. "I haven't set one of those up in ages! I know just the thing, too!"

Susana spoke up. "Actually, just the honeymoon. We'll be getting married locally."

"Are you?" The lady seemed disappointed. "Where?"

"We have our eye on a non-denominational ceremony at Buckroe Beach, but are open to other ideas," I said.

"No church wedding?"

I coughed as Susana gave the answer, "It's against his religion." Gods, I was marrying a comedian.

Aletha Dallas raised her eyebrows at that then shrugged. "That's not the strangest thing I've ever heard, young lady." She flipped open a travel magazine and scanned the pages. "So where were you thinking of going? And when? And how long?"

"We're looking at a spring wedding," I said, thankful that I hadn't been drinking anything when Susana decided to play Evening At The Improv. "Around April. Say about two weeks of a honeymoon. What have you got then?"

The travel agent smiled and turned to her computer. "Oh, I think I have a few things that might interest you." She tapped a few keys, and then said "How does Europe sound?"

"What part?"

"Spain, France, the rest of the Mediterranean? Spring is possibly one of the best times to visit the Med, and there will be plenty of chances to shop, sight-see or just relax. There's a stop in Greece as well."

I shook my head. "Sorry, that won't work." When Susana looked at me, I said, "No need to tempt the Fates, darlin."

Comprehension dawned on Susana's face as she nodded. "Yeah, I don't think Greece will work. What else do you have?"

"Let's see," Aletha murmured, "how about Acapulco? It's a bit cliché, but I'm sure you'll have fun."

This time Susana demurred, saying "I don't think it'd be a good idea. Mexico isn't that good a place for me these days."

"You mean that thing a couple of months ago?" I said. The "thing" I spoke of was her running down a group of contract killers with the help of the DEA and FBI. She was still likely *persona non grata* as far as anything south of the border for a good while. When she nodded, I shrugged. "Sorry, Ms. Dallas."

"There are so many places under heaven and earth where we can get you, Mr. Statford that I'm not even close to discouraged!" There were a few more taps on her keyboard. "Ah! Here's a great one! We call this one the Slow Boat To China. One of our---"

"No!" Susana and I said together. I continued, "No, thank you. We're kind of soured about the Orient, ma'am." I didn't want to mention the fact that my name was likely on a hit list or two after earlier in the year, and the Triads had a long memory. Those are the kinds of things you don't share with your travel agent, I don't care how nice they are. It would have a rather detrimental effect on such a business relationship.

"Well, then," Aletha said, "how about keeping it domestic? Would New Orleans grab you?"

Now there was an idea. I tried to think of anything that might cause a problem around that area, and couldn't think of anything. I could have asked Larry, my resident knowledge spirit and sidekick, but I had given him some deserved time off to do whatever it was disembodied spirits who were six thousand years old do when they weren't dealing with temperamental private detectives who needed a translation of early Sumerian script to keep some stupid mortal from bringing forth the incarnation of Ereshkigal, an ancient goddess of the dead who had a knack for being violent. Not like "I'll kick your shins" violent, but more like "I will lay waste to all creatures in my sight with glee and abandon" violent. Not a nice Sumerian goddess, to be sure.

So, the Big Easy sounded like my kind of thing. No dodging Triad kill-squads, no drug-crazed crews looking for payback, no monsters of the Greco-Roman kind. Just a great vacation, a quiet but fun wedding, and a wonderful relaxing honeymoon. I couldn't see any kind of bad things happening down there. I mean, it's damned near one of the most fun places on the face of the earth.

My brain thought the words before I could stop it: What could possibly go wrong?

"I think we might have a winner, Ms. Dallas," I said, looking over at Susana for confirmation.

She nodded, a smile on her face. "I believe we do."

"Fantastic!" Aletha Dallas clapped her hands in delight. I think she liked the idea more than we did. "It's absolutely gorgeous! You'll love it." That's when she went into the best sales job I've seen and heard. Ever. Of all time. I kept track of most of it, but by the time it was over, I couldn't wait to have my family and friends watch me get hitched at the end of April. Andrew Carnegie couldn't have done better.

I shrugged. "Well, then, let's get it scheduled." Susana smiled, which made me feel like Captain America. Word of advice, guys: When your lady is happy, your life is happy. Trust me on this one.

Before we left, Ms. Dallas made sure the reservations and the arrangements were sent to both mine and Susana's email, which, she assured us with a conspiratorial wink, would make sure no one, meaning me, would forget to send them to everyone else. I even laughed at it, because she was likely right; I would have completely let them slip my mind, and gotten read the riot act for forgetting. It wouldn't have been the first time.

As we made our way to the car, I was inordinately chipper. "See? That wasn't so hard. Told you I had it taken care of."

The look I got from the light of my life was enough to keep me quiet for the next few miles.

Chapter Three

Without a doubt, one of the toughest things to plan is a wedding. Anyone who says that there's nothing to planning one should be discounted immediately as a liar, a complete lunatic, or both. For the record, it's usually both. Between catering, hotel rooms, plane tickets, and every godsdamned miniscule thing that could possibly go wrong if it isn't taken care of that freaking instant, I began to wonder who in the name of whatever gods of sanity there was would want to get married in the first place. Seriously, there are invasions of foreign countries that are less difficult, and are quite a bit less hazardous for all concerned.

The bittersweet news was that the guest list wasn't going to be as full as we had originally planned. Though that cut down on possible things going wrong, it meant I would be without my best friends Jim McPherson and Harley Blackwater. I had known both for years, and they had been probably the greatest pair of guys I had had the pleasure to meet in my life. Mac was a cop, a newly-promoted lieutenant, to be exact, in the Newport News police department in Virginia. We had known each other before he had joined the force and I had become a private detective. The two of us had kept in touch, and every so often over the years Mac would send a case my way that smacked of the weirdness. Once he had made detective, we had worked together more often. We weren't much alike, physically; I was stocky while he had a runner's physique. He was blonde while I had dark brown hair. He was a bit taller than I was and could be very serious. For years, I had envied Mac and his domestic life, with a wife and two kids, the picket fence, and the seemingly picturesque life it implied. Of course, if he had had to go through these planning sessions, he bloody well earned that picturesque life.

Harley was the medical examiner and coroner for the cities of Hampton and Newport News, and was a full-blooded Indian. He told me he hated being called a Native American, as it was about as ridiculous a term as someone could devise. As far as he knew, he had said once, there had been no native Americans; his people had come over the land bridge. If labels were so important to people, they could label him as a member of the Seneca tribe. If that didn't do it for them, they could shove it where their brains were. Harley Blackwater cut an imposing figure at well over six feet tall, and he moved with the grace that belied his size. He was an amazing tracker and a gifted forensic pathologist who wore so many hats for the underfunded police department that his business card should have had chapter headings.

I would miss him and Mac for not being able to make it, as Mac would be in Fresno for a police conference, and Harley had a tribal matter to attend to during that week. It was just bad timing all around, but I understood since it was my fault for not setting up the time correctly. I think during the five months leading up to the trip, the four words that passed my lips most often were "I forgot" and "I'm sorry."

The other four words were "Yes, I'm a dumbass," but why add to the total?

It was just as well, even though I was supposed to have input, I did the very smart thing and kept my trap shut. The only thing I had been put in charge of was making sure I didn't forget to show up at my bachelor party.

Gods… My bachelor party. You really want to know who your friends are, let them plan a bachelor party. Your real friends are the ones who are sitting next to you in a jail cell going "Damn, that was fun," and laughing about it, while your fiancée is on her way to bail you out. Your best friends are the ones who don't let your silly ass get caught in the first place no matter how crazy things get.

And the people who crash that party? Well, they care, in their own special way, and they do say it's the thought that counts. That thought can sometimes count for twenty years in the Pits of Tartarus, of course, but hey, at least they showed they care, in some twisted, perverse and utterly insane way.

Because we had changed the venue of the wedding, Susana and I had decided any parties of the bachelor or bachelorette kind would be done and over with before we headed to New Orleans. This made some excellent sense, as Susana could get herself out of trouble with the law, and Mac and Harley could keep me out of the clink if things got too out of hand. Of course, considering I didn't drink, Mac considered chocolate milk exotic, and the only time Harley ever used alcohol was cleaning his instruments at the morgue, the likelihood of anything untoward happening was as close to zero as humanly possible. It also made anything approaching what some folks would call "fun" impossible, which was just fine by me. Excitement was not something I went looking for, since it seemed to have no problem finding me.

Maybe I'll talk about the bachelor party later. What happened that night is something that all concerned were sworn to secrecy about. There is no way I'll ever forget that party, but I won't describe it. Not yet at least. Suffice it to say, there were new laws on the books both on Earth and in the Conclave because of it.

And I still have no idea what the cow on the ceiling was for.

Anyway, as March became April and early April became late April, it became apparent that I would get to meet my future in-laws in New Orleans. I had never met them before, and only heard rumors of their existence, let alone how they were. It wasn't for lack of trying; Susana seemed to have taken an active role in keeping me from learning anything more about them than she had a mom and dad who lived in Texas. They might or might not have had other children, and might convert oxygen into carbon dioxide, but even that was in doubt, as she had told me nothing. That she had told me nothing concerned me.

So I did the only thing I could do: I asked her.

We were in bed when I brought up the subject, the moonlight sliding through the slanted blinds. Susana was lying on my chest, her head on my shoulder. It was a good, comforting weight, one I had gotten used to feeling. I did my best to be subtle about it, because, everyone knows, I'm a master of subterfuge.

I cleared my throat. "When am I meeting your family?" See? Subtle.

Susana stiffened against me, the nails of her left hand digging into my chest, and considering she had just gotten them done, they hurt like hell. I stifled a grunt of pain as I waited for her to relax. After a few seconds, she did, her nails no longer buried in my flesh, and without looking at me, she answered. "The first of May."

"Two days after the wedding?" I let out an involuntary chuckle, which earned me another clawing. "Hey, ease up on that." My fingers traced down her back trying to get her to open up. "Why?"

"Do we have to have this conversation now?" I could detect a note of pleading in her voice, but I had to know the whole truth.

"Yeah, we do." I took a deep breath and, looking down at the top of her head, I asked the question that had plagued me ever since I had asked her to marry me. "Is it because you're embarrassed of me?"

Of every possible reaction, the one I didn't expect was the one I got: laughter. "Embarrassed of you? Are you fucking kidding me?" Susana looked up at me then, propping herself up on her elbow. "*Gringo*, if I was embarrassed of you, you wouldn't be in this bed and I sure as hell wouldn't be wearing this on my finger." She held up the engagement ring, the diamond catching the moonlight. Susana gently laid her hand back on my chest. "It's my family that I'm embarrassed of."

Oh boy. "So you told them the ceremony was the first of May rather than the last of April. Why?"

"You don't know them, Tommy." Susana had opened up to me on a few things before, and there were no secrets between us. If there were, they were the kinds of secrets that were buried in the deep part of the soul, and she would tell me if and when she was damned good and ready. "You know why I'm a Newport News cop?" I shook my head. "Because I couldn't be a Brownsville cop without either busting my dad or working for him."

"Why's that?"

Susana took a deep breath before laying her head back on my chest. She spoke into the darkness, her words a constant vibration. "Brownsville isn't exactly the garden spot of the Rio Grande Valley, let alone Texas. It's a hot and terrible place, right on the border between Texas and Mexico. My family is from there, my mom and dad at least. My brother and I were born here."

I figured saying anything would be a bad idea, so I kept my mouth shut and let her continue.

"My father is a powerful man, Tommy. He built up from nothing, barely able to read or write, just like Don Corleone in that stupid movie you watch every time it comes on." I chuckled involuntarily; Susana knew my admiration of Al Pacino. "From what I read, he was brutal, calculating, even if he wasn't book-smart. He fixed that and graduated from the university in Nuevo Leòn with honors. My dad paid for it by doing whatever was asked of him by his *patron*.

"Brutal and calculating and efficient, that was my dad. He killed and lied and robbed his way to the top of the heap, displacing his own *patron* and taking over. They still haven't found all the parts, by the way. He takes over before the body is even cold." Susana let out a small laugh, though there was no humor in it. "And what did he do as soon as he was in charge? At the ripe old age of twenty-seven, he buys papers for him and his wife to be American citizens, to 'expand the business', as he put it. Murder, smuggling, extortion, making people and things disappear, procuring 'items' for the right people. That was my papa's business he 'inherited'" she twisted the word with a sneer, "from his *patron* after putting a bullet through his heart."

"How'd you find that out?" I couldn't help the question.

"I'm a cop, I'm my father's daughter, and I don't like unanswered questions, especially from my own family. There were wiretaps that he thought he had buried that I found." She sighed again. "My father can be thorough when he wants to be, but so can I. When he moved to Brownsville, it was a dump. The only thing of note in the place was a prison, and even that was more a work farm than anything. Nothing grows there, but my papa knew what could make Brownsville itself grow.

"He started off light, getting border jumpers to bring over money that was laundered in Monterrey. He would have the cash strapped to the mule in brown paper, and never worry about the mule getting into it. My papa had made it well-known what would happen to anyone who looked in the special packs." Bitterness washed over her words. "He never ran drugs, so he had that going for him, which was nice. It allowed him a bit of legitimacy, I think, at least in his own mind."

She pushed herself up and swung her legs over on the edge of the bed. Her hair hid her face as she put her elbows on her knees. Her voice filtered from behind the mass of hair, lightly muffled but still understandable. "My papa thought he was helping people make a life for themselves in the States, maybe. Thing is, usually he was bringing over about five million a year on average. Kind of shoots the whole charitable 'helping the poor people' image all to hell, doesn't it?"

I turned on my side and gently traced her spine with my fingers. After studying her for a moment, I sighed. "So your dad is the godfather of the Mexican mafia, huh?" Her head nodded. "Wow. So I guess I should be on my best behavior."

Susana swept her hair from her face in a violent gesture and glared at me incredulously. "That's it? I tell you my father made an art of killing those who got in his way, controls millions of dollars of real estate, decides the fate of everyone living within a hundred miles of Brownsville and ninety percent of Mexico, and would have no problem ordering someone to put a bullet in your head if you displeased him, and all you can say is you should behave?"

"I've dealt with gods, demons, devils and psychotic spirits," I answered, a smile forming on my face. "I've gone face to face with an archangel wielding a blazing freaking sword and lived. I beat down a no-shit mummy with a godsdamned leg bone to save my nephew. One of my best friends is the master of assassins for the east coast of the United States. On the scale of 'Things I'm Scared Of', your dad is likely not the worst thing I'll ever deal with in this lifetime." I laughed. "Besides, I figure if I keep you happy, he'll be cool with me."

That brought a snort of laughter. "My papa is 'cool' with nobody, *gringo*."

I pulled her back to me. "Babe, call him and let him know the right day for the wedding. I would like the chance to meet him before I meet you at the end of the aisle."

Her body wrapped around mine, and I could feel her heart beating against my chest. "He won't like it. He'll know I lied."

Kissing the top of her head, I squeezed her tightly. "Just tell him I gave you the wrong date. I'm a guy. We forget things. It'll be fine."

You know, those last three words should join the forbidden phrase "What could possibly go wrong?" as never to be spoken by anyone. Gods know I jinx myself enough.

Chapter Four

Have you ever been to a party that has gone on way longer than anyone could possibly imagine, and people are still coming in, to the point that it's like a never-ending sea of guests? Where the music is constant, the alcohol flows like a tidal wave, the cops don't even try stopping anything less than bodily harm and pretty much everyone thinks everyone else is awesome? How about a party the size of three city blocks where you see people in Halloween costumes in mid-July rubbing elbows and other body parts with partygoers wearing tie and tails? How about where the gift for exposing yourself is a set of cheap plastic beads? Where the press of humanity from all sides is unceasing, the voices are raised in either chanting for flashing or singing a song from the Eighties? Where you don't care about any of that going on because you are having so much fun you know you wish you could live there, and if you did live there, you would need three jobs just to make sure you had a sufficient bail fund for all the trouble you happily get into?

If you haven't, fear not: New Orleans is at worst a plane ride away, and it's worth it.

The flight had been kind to the seven of us traveling to Louis Armstrong International Airport, which was a blessing. I hated flying, but accepted that driving to the Big Easy would have been ridiculous. My mom, Aveline Statford, had sat with my sister and her family, keeping my niece and nephew entertained and out of trouble in the first class cabin. Susana kept my mind off such things as plunging into the ground at five hundred miles an hour, which was always a distinct possibility in a plane, as was the engines exploding and sending us to meet our respective makers. There was also the likelihood of Pazuzu, a Babylonian demon of the wind variety, swatting us out of the sky just because someone pissed in his corn flakes.

Like I said, I don't like flying. I have my reasons.

Thankfully, we landed with no incident, got our bags with a minimum of fuss, and made our way to the rental car place. We had rented two cars, a Chevy SUV for me and Susana, and a big old Lincoln Navigator for the rest of the family. My nephew Jacob was still on the small side, so he needed a car seat, and my sister was still a bit protective of him. Understandable, considering he had almost not made it through his first month of life.

As we drove east on Interstate 10, I felt a bit of peace flow through me. I thought to myself that this must be what the normal people feel like. No race against the clock, no sense of doom and gloom pouring through every waking moment, and no team of hitmen (mundane or otherwise) breathing down my neck trying to retire me the hard and fast way. Susana and I held hands all the way down the Interstate, even when we got stuck in a traffic jam that looked about fifty thousand miles long. The Tahoe I was driving had air conditioning, unlike the Beauty, so we were comfortable the entire two hours it took to get to the hotel.

Stephen King once wrote that true love is boring, and believe me, he's right. It's boring to everyone who isn't directly involved in it. For the two people involved, though, there's nothing boring or dull about it. It's love, and there's very little that can change their minds. Objectively, though, it was admittedly a bit of drudgery, but only because I was more used to shooting it out with hired guns or getting into a fistfight with the chosen one of a war god. However, it was because the exercise of driving a rented car to a vacation and honeymoon was so mundane that made it novel and exciting for me. You can compare it to someone who has spent years in a high stress environment like air-traffic control and never taken a day off suddenly getting a week away from everything involving the job. The ability to be able to get up and get a drink without worrying that some horribly terrible catastrophe is going to happen the second you stand is probably as close to bliss as someone like that can get with their clothes on and not ingesting some mind-altering substance.

I didn't mean to segue into the wild blue yonder like that; it's just important for people to understand that the boring and mundane for some people is paradise for people like me, who were always on the ragged edge, the first and usually only line of defense against the forces of evil, chaos and assholes that wanted to turn the world into a cinder or their own personal charnel house.

After so bloody long throwing my body, my mind, my soul against the darkness and the pain, it was about godsdamned time I got a break going my way.

Making our way through the packed Pontchartrain Expressway brought us within sight of the location of the longest running party in the history of the United States. We threaded our way through a veritable sea of cars past Louisiana State University and then took a left down Canal Street. Another left sent us down Chartres Street, which had so many museums and shops that, though they had been rebuilt only a few years prior, looked like we were on the set of *Interview With A Vampire*.

I had been to New Orleans once before while on leave before becoming the Keeper, and even through hurricanes and corrupt government officials had gone through repeatedly, the beauty of the Big Easy hadn't faded. Chartres Street was a narrow thoroughfare, especially from the fact it was a one-way street and people seemed to enjoy parking five feet away from the curb. We passed the Historic New Orleans Collection at the Williams Research Center on our right, and the Louisiana Supreme Court building on the left. The neon from the storefronts on the right was visible even in the daylight, ruining some of the magic of yesteryear, but adding in its own sense of modern times. New Orleans was a study in contrasts, where old and new didn't clash but melded almost seamlessly into an amalgam that shouldn't have been natural but was. I felt at home in a way that was alien to me, like I had been missing something so much I didn't know it was gone.

As I turned into the parking garage for the hotel, I chuckled. Susana asked what was so funny. "Just thinking how it is to find something you didn't know was gone, and how good a feeling it is."

Susana raised an eyebrow. "You are so weird sometimes, Tommy."

"You aren't marrying me for my normalcy, darlin."

"Yeah, because you sure as hell don't have any of that. Here's a spot." She pointed out an unlikely pair of parking spaces next to each other, which had to be rare as hen's teeth. "Looks like we got lucky."

"Certainly seems that way. Let's wait for the others to get out and ready to go in. You know it takes Hannah forever." We sat in silence for a moment as my brother-in-law maneuvered the huge SUV into parking space with a skill most would ascribe to a professional valet. While he parked, I broke the silence. "So when are they meeting us?"

Susana instantly knew who I meant. "You just won't give up, will you, *gringo*?" She heaved a sigh and said, "Papa, Mama and my brother Paolo will be meeting us in the hotel bar tomorrow."

"Tomorrow? Two days before we tie the knot?" I smiled at her. "You don't think that's cutting it a bit close?"

Through gritted teeth, Susana said, "You have no idea what I went through to keep him from flying up to Virginia last week. It was a close thing, and he probably would have brought back your head to put on his mantelpiece."

"For what?" I chuckled. "Babe, he's not really that bad, is he?"

Susana rolled her eyes and ran a distracted hand through her hair. "*Jesucristo*, were you not listening before? Tommy, my papa has killed people, with absolutely no hesitation. Sure, he's arranged to have them killed, but has no problem doing the job himself. I left Texas for just that reason. He takes insults to him or his family very personally." Her hand covered mine and squeezed. "He don't mess around."

"In case you hadn't noticed, neither do I." I smiled easily, but inwardly, I promised to show her dad the deference and respect he deserved, and not because he was likely a stone killer. It would be due to him helping bring Susana to the world. For that I would be ever grateful to him.

Of course, the not-getting-killed part did have a place in that thinking. I'm crazy, not stupid.

The bellhop or porter or whatever they call them these days came up with a ginormous luggage carrier, rolling on four wheels and rattling like the cups of hungry prisoners in cages. I popped the back and started unloading bags, mindful that my brother-in-law Arthur had already gotten his Navigator unloaded while Susana and I had been talking. The carrier rattled a lot less with about twenty tons of suitcases weighing it down, and apparently made it hard for the bellhop to push. Arthur and I smiled a bit as we gave the guy a boost, getting the carrier trundling along at a decent speed.

"Do you think we have enough clothing for the week?" My sister Jennifer looked concerned. Where I had gotten the rugged looks, she had gotten the fashion model genes, with long wavy dark brown hair, clear skin and a naturally thin figure. Her usually smooth brow was furrowed, no doubt trying to calculate just what we were missing while keeping an eye on Hannah and Jacob. "I don't think we brought enough underwear for the babies."

That elicited a drawn-out "Mooooooooom!" from Hannah, and I didn't know which the little girl had found more offensive: her mother talking about her underwear or lack thereof, or being called a baby. My niece was nine years old, precocious, smart as a whip and exceptionally protective of her baby brother, who rolled his eyes and laughed at his sister's embarrassment. Both had lighter brown hair, a shade midway between Arthur and Jennifer's color. Hannah had hazel eyes while Jacob's eyes had more of a bluish tint to the iris. The young boy was much smaller and very skinny, even though he was only two years Hannah's junior. That slimness was due to him being very sick when he was born, a condition I helped to fix. The sight of the twin necklaces around their necks warmed my heart, even as it made the healed stab wounds on my leg and in my side throb in memory.

"Hannah, I only worry because I'm your mother," Jen said, her tone of admonishment about as fearsome as milk. I knew Hannah loved the doting, and only made a fuss because it made Jacob laugh. "When you have kids of your own, you'll understand."

"Hannah a mommy?" Jacob howled with laughter, making baby noises and kissing faces at his sister. "That would be awesome!" he cried, nearly doubling over from laughing.

The object of the mirth stopped suddenly and put her hands on her hips. Rounding on her brother, Hannah gave the look that would one day rival the Look my mom had once upon a time given me and my sister. "Yes, it will! I'll be a great mommy, and if you keep laughing, you're so gonna get it!"

I took that moment to step in; Arthur was busy with the luggage carrier which was dealing with one of Newton's laws, namely the one about objects in motion tending to stay in motion. "Okay, Princess Shelanna, Ruler of the Midgets," I intoned, going to her to nudge her along, "no bodily harm will be threatened against your loyal subjects, even the short ones." I gave Jacob the Eye, making sure he knew that he needed to tone it down a bit and get inside the hotel. "Move it out, or I won't be able to protect you both from the real threat."

As Hannah started to walk again, she looked up at me. "What threat?"

"Yeah, Uncle Tommy," Jacob echoed. "What threat?"

Hooking a thumb over my shoulder, I indicated my mother, who was serenely walking behind us. "That lady right there. I'd rather juggle chainsaws than make her mad."

Jacob's voice quivered slightly as he asked, "Really?"

Both children looked at Mom with a wide-eyed wonder as she passed, silence emanating from them and a slight smile on my mother's face. Aveline Statford turned her head to the left to take in both of them with her gaze and said simply, "Really."

Jacob and Hannah quickly took my hands and stayed very quiet. I gave them a squeeze and a quick wink, so they would smile back. The two children looked up at me questioningly for a moment then relaxed when I gave a toothy grin, to let them know I was kidding.

For the record, no, I wasn't kidding.

I guided my two charges to their mother, who was worrying about something else that I didn't quite catch. After telling my sister to relax a bit, I made my way over to Susana, who was at the registration desk.

Really, though, calling the lobby of the hotel just a lobby was a disservice to it, as it was gorgeous. It truly was like some amalgamation of mid-eighteenth century plantation and twenty-first century modern era design, with long flowing staircases circling around at the far end of the lobby, a mellow glow to the wood as it spiraled up to the second floor. Directly across from the grand pair of staircases were different types of doors, all glass and metal, two sets revolving, one automatic and two old-fashioned pulling types, allowing entrance from Chartres Street. The walls were a very light yellow, almost the color of ancient parchment. Spaced between old paintings of landowners and scenes of decades long past were huge monitors showing the weather, amenities, traffic reports and tour schedules. The floor was marble, the patterns of blacks and greys and whites not-quite-random, and absolutely amazing, giving the impression of much more space than there actually was. Uniformed men and women stood by to assist anyone who needed help.

Across from the front desk, a monolithic chunk of carved mahogany that fairly hummed with age and regality, was the entrance to the bar and grille. It was dark and nearly impossible to see inside from where I stood. There seemed to be some kind of sporting event going on, given the amount of noise coming from the wide open glass doors, which included cheering, catcalls, and language not suitable for those under the age of thirty. I shook my head and smiled, even though my sister sent a disapproving look in the direction of the bar after the eighth time the word "Sumbitch!" was shouted. Though Jennifer did use harsh language with the skill of Joe Pesci dropping an anvil on his foot, she was careful about using it around the kids. I decided not to make an issue of it; after all, this was my pre-wedding honeymoon. The last thing I wanted to do was borrow trouble.

That was of course when the dying man crashed through the front doors.

I mean that literally, as glass flew everywhere, cutting several people with flying slivers. None of my family was near, which I took as a blessing of luck, but it seemed to be a near thing. The crash of breaking glass had sliced through the crowded lobby like a chainsaw through smoke, bringing everyone's attention to the savaged form staggering to and fro. Guests shrank away from the man's questing right hand as it clutched at the air, reaching for something the walking corpse would never find. Blood dripped from the fingertips of one hand, falling to the marble floor in a crimson rain. I took in the sight of the man's silk suit, once the color of vanilla ice cream and now more streaked with raspberry lines. Rips and tears in the clothing showed where the glass had scraped up pale flesh, the lines on the skin dark with blood. The man's left hand was at his stomach and seemed to be clutching something, even as he staggered forward on savaged legs.

My eyes tracked up from his empty right hand to his face, and I wish I hadn't. His eyes were gone. It hadn't been gentle removal either, as the empty sockets pumped blood down his cheeks like crimson tears. The sounds coming from his throat were almost inhuman; it was like his voicebox had broken and the only noises he could make were choked coughs that were wet with tears or saliva. What was worse was he seemed aware of what was happening as he staggered for anything that made a sound. For ten eternal seconds after the crash through the glass door, the walking dead man stumbled toward anyone who gasped or cried out. My mind filled with disgust and horror at the knowledge that this poor bastard knew exactly what was happening to him, and that his life was ending drop by drop, step by step.

Without knowing I was doing it, I ran toward him, knowing he was a dead man walking but refusing to just stand there and do nothing. Dimly I heard myself call out for Susana to call the paramedics while I tried in vain to reach him before he fell forward. Irrationally, I thought if I caught him before he hit the floor, he might be able to be saved. A ridiculous idea, but when there's a man bleeding from what seems like a hundred thousand places, any hope is better than no hope.

His ruined face with those empty sockets swiveled toward the sound of my shouts and his mouth opened in a rictus of a hopeful grin. My trained eye slowed down the whole scene, completely independent of my wishes. As the lips bulled back in a smile, I saw black stumps of what might once have been teeth, seemingly rotting before my eyes. The sockets seemed to fill with pus, yellow and jellied and pushing aside the blood. I watched the poor sorry bastard drop first to one knee, then both knees. When I was a scant fifteen feet away from him, he swayed and fell forward onto his chest with a sickening splat, his face also striking the cold marble floor. It was the sound of a thick steak, freshly cut, smacking down onto the wooden cutting board. Blood mixed with yellowish ooze and began forming a pool around the man's head and upper body. I stopped short, disgusted by the sight as time returned to normal.

I stood there, the perimeter of the pool of body fluids stopping a foot from my sneakers. The dead man had made it within six feet of me, or I from him, when he succumbed to his wounds. I circled the corpse, looking at the ruined form with its cuts and scrapes and horrid gashes. The relatively unscathed back of the man seemed to sprout bloody lines underneath the coat, even though there were no obvious marks on the clothing itself. There was no movement from the body, which I found both comforting and odd. It was comforting because, after such a violent death, I never wanted to see the body move again. It was odd because, after such a violent death, there should have been muscle spasms or a death rattle or something, especially after that faceplant into the floor. It was just sudden and instant death.

I looked over to Susana, nodding her head silently. I took that to mean that she had called the paramedics. Glancing over where my sister was, I saw that she was with Arthur, and they both had the kids as far as possible from the scene. Jacob kept trying to peek, but Hannah was wise to what was going on and kept her little brother from getting more of an eyeful than he needed. Mom stood near a table, talking quietly into a cell phone. Her eyes seemed to be tracing the scene and though I couldn't hear her words, I figured she was relaying something to her agency. She's nothing if not efficient and adaptable.

That left me nearly within arm's-reach of a corpse that appeared to be continuing to bleed. I grimaced as I crouched down on the left side of the dead man, his left hand underneath him, seemingly clutching his stomach. Where the skin was not streaked with blood or covered in cloth there was a mottled, almost marbled look. What was more, it looked like the body was deflating, draining of volume. The best way to explain it would be like a water balloon draining slowly, with just enough left inside to form a rudimentary body. The overall effect was disturbing, to put it mildly.

"Gods," I muttered. "What a fucking mess." I crouched down to get a better look at the body. Unfortunately, I also got a good whiff of the corpse, which had evacuated its bowels in extremis. That scent coupled with the pus coming from the eyes and the rot coming from the mouth, along with other rank smells emanating from the body, clenched my stomach tight. I was glad I had skipped the TV dinner the airline had offered on the way down to New Orleans; I had no desire to see it again.

As I was so close to the ruined body, I caught the scent of some kind of herb or flower coming from it. The spicy scent was nearly trampled by the gory smells that made me nearly lose my light breakfast of juice and toast. I couldn't quite place it, though I knew that I knew it. It danced on the tip of my awareness, and all my mind could come up with was Cheech and Chong. It made no sense, so I pushed it away for the moment.

I heard steps behind me on the marble, steady like clockwork. The steps originated from the bar and grille, which had gone quiet as a tomb like the whole lobby. Only thirty seconds or so had passed since the man had fallen, and I was the only one brave or stupid enough to approach. "Stay back, man," I warned over my shoulder, not taking my eyes off the body. "You don't need to get any closer." When the pace didn't falter, I turned a bit more, holding a hand up. "I said back the hell off. Paramedics are coming, and as few people need to be exposed to this as possible." That got whoever was coming to slow down, but not stop. "Dude, the cops are already going to be pissed at me; you don't want them pissed at you. Keep your ass where it is." At that, the steps stopped a good ten feet away, allowing me to focus on the shitstorm at hand.

With the interloper held off, I lowered my hand and whispered a name. "Larrisimus." Just like that, Larry appeared to my right. He was dressed in a brown cassock that looked made of silk rather than sackcloth. As he raised his head, Larry looked down at me, and he seemed mightily annoyed.

"Thomas, I thought the ceremony was not for another three days," the spirit said by way of greeting. "Do not tell me you and Susana---" He trailed off as he saw the corpse. "Oh dear."

"That's one way to put it," I whispered, pulling out my phone. I fiddled with it, and started talking into it like I was recording something, though my words were directed to Larry. "He crashed through the glass doors like they were paper, tore the hell out of himself, and collapsed on the godsdamned floor."

Larry's cassock melted into a two-button Giorgio Armani suit colored a mellow purple. He gained a half-inch of height from the black leather shoes that formed on his feet. After he was properly garbed, he silently circled the body, looking both cultured and disgusted. "Oh, Thomas, this is revolting! What happened after he collapsed?"

"The victim began to… deflate," I said, my words failing me. "His left hand was clutched against his stomach the entire time, like he was going to throw up. Even after he came through the glass, he kept holding his midsection."

"Vomiting was the least of his worries, I can guarantee that." Larry lowered a hand down close to the blood, then drew back with a hiss. "Oh dear."

I broke character and asked the obvious. "What is it?"

The spirit's mouth was drawn tightly as he made the pronouncement. "There is magic in this blood. Dark magic."

"Bullshit, Larry," I hissed. "There's no such thing." Even as I said the words, though, I knew I was wrong. After all, I dealt with gods and devils and everything in between. Saying magic didn't exist would have been the height of insanity on my part.

"Be that as you believe, Thomas, this is the result of a death curse." Larry took a step away from the pool of bodily fluids. "This man was hit and hit hard by some kind of curse from a *houngan.*"

"A witch doctor?" I narrowed my eyes. "I thought they weren't allowed to do something like this. Something about being against the Law of Voodoo."

"Apparently, someone does not care much for the law, and you are talking to yourself again." Larry pointed casually behind me at the small but growing crowd of people gawking at me as I seemed to be having a conversation on my own. Among them were a couple of bellhops, what looked like a manager, and a rather patrician-looking dark-skinned man staring at me.

"Sir?" The guy who looked like he ran the hotel during the daylight hours stammered. He had a passing resemblance to Tim Curry in his younger days. "Are you well? Is he---?"

"Yeah, he is. Sorry. I talk to myself sometimes in high-stress situations," I smiled tightly, as harmlessly as I could. "Everyone copes differently, right?"

"Are you a policeman?"

"I work with the cops, actually." I didn't bother showing my consultant ID as it was in my office hundreds of miles to the northeast. I looked over his curly hair. "Anyway, here come the paramedics."

Threading their way through the swelling crowd were several members of the local ambulance crews, and that gave me a chance to back off and away. They'd find out the same thing I did, that the guy was dead and there wasn't a godsdamned thing they could do about it. I put it out of my head for the moment as I made my way over to Susana, who was helping to run interference with the kids along with Arthur and Jennifer. Mom was off to the side still, talking into her phone with a low voice but an animated face.

"What is it, *gringo*?" Susana asked, her eyes worried as she turned to me.

"Don't know," I shrugged. "Not my job, babe. The locals can handle it."

She raised an eyebrow to me and then nodded. "Don't want to get involved, huh?"

I sighed and reached down to pick up Jacob. Though smaller than his sister, he could be heavy when he wanted. "You know I'm getting married to you in a couple of days, right? I'm officially on vacation, and I'd like to have some bit of relaxation." Shifting Jacob from my right shoulder to my left to block his view of the festivities behind me, I said, "Besides, I have to get ready to meet your folks, and the last thing I want to do is make a bad impression." Susana's eyes widened. "I mean, what if I said the wrong thing at the wrong time?"

A new voice, coming from only a few feet behind me, sliced across my words

"For example, telling your possibly future father-in-law to, how did you put it, 'back the hell off' or to keep his ass where it is?" It was a deep voice, full of command. In only a single sentence, it told me exactly what its owner thought of me, and if I tried really hard, I might one day reach the level of rancid worm shit. "I assure you that, *Señor*, would not be something you would want to say to me."

I closed my eyes and shook my head slightly, trying to ponder just how bad it was going to go for me. It got instantly worse as Jacob piped up with "Hey, Uncle Tommy, who's the old guy? He talks funny."

Kids just say the darnedest things.

Chapter Five

First impressions are important. Don't let anyone tell you differently. If you've ever interviewed for a job and had toilet paper stuck to your shoe, you know you likely aren't getting that job. Ditto on cussing some lady out on the freeway when she cuts you off, and then meeting her for that ever-so-awkward first blind date. Of course, there's always the popular "'meet' after cursing out your future father-in-law when a walking dead man staggers through the lobby of an upscale hotel."

Don't you just hate when that happens, or is it just me?

The police and paramedics had already left by the time I got the chance to catch my bearings. Thankfully I didn't have too much trouble with the local cops, as the stories they got from everyone else jibed with mine, namely that the guy had been bleeding pretty well on his own by the time I made his acquaintance. I gave the best account I could, omitting anything involving voodoo and spirits only I could see. I was due for a tuxedo jacket in a couple of days, not a strait one.

The question and answer session was a lovely hour interrogation by the locals, who spent fifteen seconds trying to bully me until they found out that I was traveling with a cop and two lawyers. Even though Arthur was based out of Virginia, the words "Attorney General's office" carried a lot of weight. Susana talked to them as well, relaying in terse cop-speak who I was and what happened. I still had to give the same story five times, which annoyed me, though I didn't allow it to show. There was no way I wanted to give them any more reason to keep me on ice than "person of interest" allowed.

By the time I sat down and had more than two seconds to think, I was completely spent. I wanted to do nothing more than to go up to the room, take a long hot shower, and sleep for a full day right through. Maybe that would get the sight of those empty orbs out of my memory, or at least make them more distant so I didn't see them every time I closed my eyes.

Of course, I might as well have wished for the moon, as Susana's father purposefully strode up to where I sat, stood firm as he crossed his arms over his chest, and said simply, "Well?"

Utterly befuddled, I looked up at him. He was not a tall man, maybe a shade taller than my five-feet-ten, but was well-kept by a body that had seen either years of hard work in the field or the gym, even both. I figured him to be about in his mid-sixties, his hair gone to silver with black streaks rather than vice-versa. The mustache and beard combination were expertly trimmed, salt and pepper in the whiskers, framing a mouth set in stony disapproval. His clothes were spotless silk, in the neighborhood of five hundred dollars just for the short-sleeved shirt. Distractedly, I wondered what a shirt with long sleeves would have cost.

His eyes brought me back to reality, though. They were completely unreadable. I looked into those black pools and saw only a reflection of myself. I had dealt with creatures with that kind of gaze before, and it never went well for anyone. It was the look of a man who hadn't quite decided what to do with this new thing in front of him. Crush it? Wait and see? Wait and then crush it anyway? I was the ant, and he was the kid with the magnifying glass on a hot summer day.

I cleared my throat, preparing to wow him with my rapier wit. "Well what?" See, wasn't that rapier-like?

"I believe you owe me an apology."

"I'm sorry I kept you from stepping in a pool of disgusting bodily fluids?" I was thoroughly confused as to why I was supposed to be giving an apology.

He raised a grey eyebrow. Like father, like daughter. "I meant about your tone with me. It was quite disrespectful."

The hammer hit the top of my head, striking the reset button on my brain. "Sir, I haven't even properly met you yet, and for that I truly am sorry. I was told we'd be meeting tomorrow."

He puffed up a bit, probably trying to just keep his sense of superiority over me. After all, I was still seated, looking up at him like he was some lord. I knew the psychology, which gave me some immunity from it. Besides, I've stared down a pissed-off war god. I don't intimidate easily. "Yes, that is true. However, I felt it better to come early, to see what kind of man is going to marry my daughter."

I chuckled a bit. "Trust me, this was not how I pictured the first meeting." Standing brought us almost eye-level, and I stuck out my hand. "Thomas Statford, sir, and it's a pleasure to finally meet you."

"Don Salvador José Iglesias y Marquez," he answered, trading a firm grip. "I admit, Mr. Statford, I did not think we would have the chance to meet before you whisked my daughter down the aisle." He gestured towards the bar, which in the late afternoon was empty for the moment. "Please come with me."

Following him, especially after Susana's words about him being a stone killer came back to mind, seemed like a really bad idea, on the order of juggling cobras. "Don Salvador, shouldn't we wait for Susana? I think she'll be done in a minute."

"What I have to say does not require her to be present, Mr. Statford. I wish only a moment."

Against my better judgment, I preceded him into the bar, which looked just like every other bar I had ever set foot in. It was dark from both the lights being low and the windows being tinted. Booths were set up along the walls and windows, with small circular tables dotting the floor. The chairs surrounding the tables were empty. The bar was empty and clean, which surprised me, and the bartender was conspicuously absent, which concerned me. One booth was not empty, and it was on the opposite side of the entrance to the bar. Seated were two people, and I was introduced with very little warning and fanfare to Susana's mother and brother.

"Mr. Statford, may I introduce my wife Maria, and my son Paolo." The lady was in her fifties and could pass for mid-thirties. Perfectly coiffed black hair, a trim figure that looked like she spent days on end in the gym and eyes glittering with intelligence behind rimless glasses, Maria Marquez was wearing something similar to her husband, though it was sleeveless and showed off her tanned arms. Manicured fingers with about three carets of various stones tapped distractedly on the table. She had her legs crossed under the table, the khaki slacks ironed to a razor crease. She nodded to me in greeting, which didn't make me feel much better, considering her eyes seemed to catalogue me in such a manner that I felt lacking in some essential way.

Paolo Marquez was either almost out of his twenties or just getting into his thirties. His full head of ebony hair was expertly cut with a left-side part. He had dark eyes like a hawk and a toothy grin that made me a bit uncomfortable to see. His shirt was unbuttoned at the top, showing off three gold chains, one of them sporting a small golden cross. A pinkie ring on his left hand had a ruby that caught the dim light and reflected it. The grin was what brought me up short, though. It was like looking at a trap that was ready to spring at a moment's notice.

"A pleasure to meet you both," I smiled tightly, not giving in to the fear in my stomach. This was definitely not how I pictured things going. However, I truly doubted that Don Salvador would introduce me to his wife and son before trying to kill me. A murderer and Mexican mafia kingpin he might have been, but I got the vibe he was at least cultured enough to get to know me before he tried to give me a severe case of death.

"Do sit, Mr. Statford," Maria smiled, the gesture dimpling her cheeks but stopping well short of her eyes. "I'm hoping we can become better acquainted."

I did so, not wanting to be rude. "Of course, ma'am. I'm hoping the same as well."

"My daughter tells me you are a private investigator," Don Salvador said, taking his own seat next to his wife. "Is that a good profession for someone wanting to start a family?"

"It pays the bills, sir," I said, and immediately regretted it. Being glib was not going to win me any bonus points. "I mean, Susana and I haven't made any concrete plans as yet about starting a family. We thought we'd have at least a honeymoon before we got that far."

"Mr. Statford," Maria interjected, "since you started your business, you have barely broken even except for the last three years." My eyes shifted to her. "In fact, your last year's return was well into the six figures. Is that normal?"

Crap. Of course they had dug into my financials. "No, ma'am, not normal. Just a very good year for me."

"So you'll go back to being nearly destitute," the Don said, his voice tight, "or will you be living off of my daughter?"

"I assure you, Don Salvador, I have no intention of living off of anyone." My words started getting clipped, as an accusation of that nature was below the belt. "I work hard to make ends meet, and I will work even harder to make sure that I'm pulling my weight in the relationship."

"Be that as it may, *señor*," Paolo spoke up for the first time, the grin never wavering, "my sister needs someone who can take care of her, and one lucky year don't really cut it."

"*Si*, this is true," Maria nodded sagely, the twinkling gone from her eyes. "How can we be sure Susana will be properly taken care of?"

So it wasn't going to be a physical assassination, but character and confidence assassination. Oh goody. The thing was, if they had thought I was going to cower under an assault like that, they obviously hadn't done the right homework on me. "Ma'am, I can give you no guarantees of the future. I can only tell you what I will do." I stood up slowly, glancing at all three in turn. "I love Susana. I wouldn't be with her if I didn't, and I sure as hell wouldn't marry her otherwise. I will do everything I can to keep her happy. She is everything to me, my whole life, my whole world." My palms were flat on the table, if only to keep the trembling in check. It was anger, not fear that made my hands want to shake. "There is nothing I won't do for her." I took a deep breath and stood up straight. "Now, if you'll excuse me, I'm going to go find my fiancée and my family and bring them in so we can all have a wonderful evening together." I pushed the chair back and began to walk away.

"You are a brave man, Mr. Statford." Don Salvador's words made me stop in my tracks. Usually those words were followed by either the sound of a gunshot or the sounds leading up to a gunshot. I braced myself for the punching sensation that a bullet caused; it wouldn't have been the first time I had been shot.

Instead, I felt a hand on my right shoulder. I looked over to see Don Salvador smiling at me. It was a tired, resigned smile, like the one someone gives when they realize that time has finally caught up with them, and they have to either let go and accept the present and future, or hold and cause the past to tear everything you ever held dear away into ashes. The Don nodded, still with that tired and accepting smile. "I see that my daughter chose well, Mr.

Statford." Taking his hand from my shoulder, he beckoned his wife and son to follow. "Let us go meet the in-laws together, *si*?"

I let out the breath I hadn't realized I had been holding. Meeting the Don's smile with my own, I said, "After you, sir, and please call me Tom."

At that, he actually laughed. "No, Tom, I don't think that will be a good idea. My daughter will want to see you first, to make sure you are still alive."

I began to walk forward, confidently at first, and then I looked over my shoulder. "Was there any doubt?"

Paolo was the one who answered. "Do you truly want the answer to that?"

Shaking my head, I responded, "You know what, let's go find Susana."

As we exited the bar, night was falling outside, and even after the horrific events of the day, I was feeling pretty good. I had met my future in-laws, and I had either convinced them of my sincerity, impressed them with my bravery, or both. Regardless, they seemed to like me, and I wasn't going to end up on a slab that night due to being a smartass.

Though my mind kept going back to the body that had crashed into what was supposed to be one of the happiest times of my life, I pushed the thoughts away. Holding Susana close after she checked me for blood or holes from meeting her family washed away any interest I had finding out about the corpse. I was on vacation; the Conclave could go get along without me for a week. Besides, not everything that had to do with the gods had to be fixed by me. *Just this once*, I prayed to whoever would bother listening, even as a joke, as Mom met Don Salvador and family, *let this pass me by. Just frigging once.*

I should have known better. In fact, I knew better. No rest for the weary.

Chapter Six

It was the magic time between day and dark, that middle ground of dusk that covered New Orleans. The sounds of revelry had already begun from Bourbon Street, home of one of the longest running parties in history. Shouts and laughter flew through the breeze like confetti, there and gone without staying too long. Electric light filtered down from the intermittently lit lampposts, casting a feeble glow that was drowned out by the bright neon coming from the storefronts. Partygoers in outlandish costumes trickled by us, some wearing regular street clothes, others wearing outfits better suited for either a nursery or a BDSM club, or both for that matter. Glass or sparks flashed in their hands, being either bottles or cigarettes, and in some cases both.

In other words, it was party time in the Big Easy, and the fun was just beginning for folks.

Jennifer and Arthur decided to stay with the kids for the night, as they were still freaked out about the incident in the lobby. I could hardly blame them, as my mind kept going back to it like a curious puppy nibbling on a bone. Hannah and Jacob were okay, which was the important thing. They hadn't seen much, or at least hadn't said anything about it. I had explained clearly to the two young children that everything was okay, that the police had taken care of things, and there was nothing to worry about. It didn't feel like a lie to me, and I felt good about that. It didn't involve me or anyone in the family, local or extended, so I couldn't have given a damn less about the dead guy. Weirdness happens around me; I accepted that and let it go. If I thought about it too long, it would likely drive me crazy. I did, however, ask Larry to keep an eye on things while we were gone. Better safe than sorry.

After giving assurances to the children and my sister and brother-in-law even more assurances that everything was fine, the remaining six of us made our way through the streets towards one of the most famous streets in America and likely the world. I took a deep breath of the night air, and though it seemed that nine out of ten people had some kind of cigarette lit, it was a clear breath, filling my lungs. It felt good to me, holding Susana's right hand as we walked past a few of the shops. Mom was on my right side, with the Don and his wife on my left. Paolo had decided to go off on his own, speaking hurried Spanish to his father and getting a disapproving glare from his mother, and I knew enough Spanish to figure out he was going to sponsor the college educations of a few of the young ladies who danced in the clubs.

Hey, I was young once, and contributed to the Exotic Dancers Education Fund on a few occasions. It was good for the economy, but bad for my wallet.

We walked along St. Peter Street for a block then took a left onto Rue Royal. We had nowhere pressing to go, though I knew we would want to get something to eat soon. I had no real desire to plunge into the mass of people we could see going farther down St. Peter towards Bourbon, at least not on a nearly empty stomach. Besides, it was much too early to get into the party. I leaned against a convenient pillar while Susana, Mom and Maria did some window-shopping. The Don and I kept up a companionable silence as the ladies chatted, Maria much more animated than when I saw her in the bar.

Don Salvador looked at me for a moment, and smiled enigmatically. When I half-smiled and tilted my head in question, the Don said, "Something you will have to get used to."

"What's that?"

"Waiting for her to get done shopping." The Don nodded toward Susana. "She would take just short of forever making a decision when it came to clothes. There was nothing she would not try on at least four times before deciding on something completely different." He looked at me. "I hope you have patience, Tom."

"Patience is something I learned a long time ago in this job, sir."

"Then you are truly blessed."

That brought a bark of laughter from me. "I said I learned it. I never said I was good at it."

"Tommy, over here!" Susana called me over to an antique shop's window. The Don followed me, laughter carrying us there.

When we got closer, Susana looked at the both of us. "What's so funny, you two?"

"You have a good man here, *mija*." The Don clapped me on the back. "Wise beyond his years."

Susana stifled laughter with a look of incredulity. "Don't let that fool you, Papa. I taught him everything he knows." She slipped her arm around mine and pulled me close. "What do you think of that?"

I followed her finger, pointing at the window, or more particularly, the specific contents of the window. My breath caught in my throat at the sight and a smile grew on my lips. It was a silver necklace, the chain itself a braid of linked chains so fine as to look like threads. The braid was made of three braided chains, each made of three braids, and each of those was made of three braids. The metal glittered in the light, the blue and red neon flashing off it. Even that craftsmanship was nothing compared to the charm hanging from it.

It was a silver cross, simple and elegant. The cross was two inches long by a little under an inch, with the limbs of the cross a scant quarter of an inch. What was on it was breathtaking. From what I could see, there was faint engraving on the silver, the lines delicately etched into the metal. As I looked closer, they seemed to change from flowing to curled to straight. Perhaps it was just a trick of the light, but it actually looked like it was changing before my eyes. The metalwork was exquisite, to say the least, as I had seen engraving like that before, done by normal humans, which made it even more awesome.

"I'm not much for jewelry, but that is probably the most beautiful necklace I've ever seen," I breathed.

"Indeed it is, Tom," the Don agreed.

To Susana, I said, "You want it, babe?"

Susana laughed, her head shaking. "That thing is just way too expensive, gringo. You don't have to buy it."

Of course, this meant I was buying it. "Be right back." I walked into the antique shop, and immediately forgot why I had gone in. My jaw dropped to my chin at what I saw. Along the walls, all the way to the ceiling was just stuff. I know that's not at all descriptive, but I am talking about shelves and hooks and stands holding such a variety of merchandise as to make a discount store jealous. I can't even begin to catalog everything I saw, and it seemed to go up higher than the roof of the shop. I could see dolls, toys, and old board games on the wall to my left, various knick-knacks adorning the right wall, and pictures and paintings covering the wall across from the entrance. Shelves were everywhere, carrying silverware, jewelry, and other trinkets with jewels winking in the dim light from the chandelier. Tables were festooned with shoes, picture frames, and books, all cracked and yellowed with age. I felt like I was in the most organized hoarder's house in the world, as everything seemed to have a proper place, and even though it looked like there was no rhyme or reason for the way all the items to have been placed, the placement made sense. The only way my mind could get it straight was organized clutter.

Amid the piles and the tables was a counter that doubled as a glass display case. The glass was shined to perfection, and the inside glowed with its own light. There were various bags that looked made of leather in the case, with leather thongs wrapped around the tops of the bags. I leaned in close to the glass, my breath steaming on the case as I tried reading the chicken scratch writing on the cards beneath each bag. A short black mannequin dressed in a shawl and patchwork dress sat in front of the case, which was a bit annoying; I wanted to see what was hidden by the mannequin. I didn't want to move it from where it was, especially since there was nowhere to move it without blocking one of the few paths through the clutter. I sighed as I tried to look over the mannequin. Unfortunately, it was right in the worst spot for me to look around and even though it was only about four and a half feet tall, it was too tall to just look over. Deciding it was a lost cause, I admitted defeat and moved on.

I had gotten two steps away when the mannequin spoke. "Help you, sonny?" it said conversationally in a high but scratchy woman's voice.

I won't say I didn't make a sound when it spoke, but to my dying day I will refuse to admit I yelped. I did jump, though, and bumped into a precariously piled stack of magazines which nearly fell before I managed to steady them. The act gave me a moment to catch my breath and my bearings. Once I was sure I wasn't going to sound like a high school kid in a horror movie, I turned to the speaker. "Sorry. You startled me."

"You thought I was party of the scenery," the woman cackled. "It's okay. Tell the truth and shame the devil, I always say!" She cackled again, her dark skin crinkling in pleasure and her bright white teeth that could only be dentures displayed as she laughed. Looking closer at her, I wasn't sure how I could have mistaken her for anything but a well-made statue. Her glasses were smoky, hiding the whites of her eyes, though I could feel her stare at me. It was a calculating and shrewd stare, taking me in and measuring me. Her mouth remained in a slight smile as she pushed herself away from the counter. I was rather amused that she hadn't been sitting in front of the counter; she was actually that short. She shuffled a few steps towards another table, this one holding small leather bags similar to what was in the case. "You be lookin for the *gris-gris*, boy?"

My mind came back to why I had come into the store in the first place. "Actually, I was looking at the necklace you have in the window." I didn't move from where I was, as the paths were only wide enough for one person, and while she was short, she wasn't exactly svelte. "My lady likes it."

The woman turned to look at me with a knowing smile. "Oh, so your lady want some silver round her neck? Gran Ibo know what women like. What men like, too. You tourists?" She continued shuffling, this time to the window where the necklace was.

"Kind of, ma'am," I answered, keeping a respectful distance. "We're getting married in a couple of days."

Gran Ibo had reached the window but froze when I had said the word "married". With the way she was standing, I couldn't see what she was doing at the window. I looked away at a couple of paintings hanging from the wall. "You marrying somebody? That sound serious." Ibo's voice was tinged with something I couldn't place. "You love her?"

"She's my world." I chuckled at the portraits. They were of a pair of severe looking men. One wore a hat that was painted half red and half black, the other looked like a character from an old James Bond film I had seen years before. I couldn't place the name or the face of the subject of the portrait, but he wore a top hat and his face was painted with a skull. Never was a big fan of Bond after Connery hung it up. "She's everything." I turned back to look at Gran Ibo.

Who happened to be standing scant inches from me, looking up at me intently with those smoky lenses. Her mouth was set in a stern line, though it was in determination rather than disapproval. I managed not to jump that time, even though her sudden appearance scared the hell out of me again.

She held up the necklace, which was even more beautiful up close. The clasp was open, the ends dangling down the sides of her upheld hand. The silver cross was bright in her palm, and the lines still seemed to move on the metal. "This a special necklace, boy." Her voice was no longer the crackle of an old lady, but the deep vibrant voice of a much younger woman. "You know what we call it?" I shook my head, dumbfounded. "We call it *Fete Twa a Mare*, and it is special. You still want it for your woman or did it catch your eye?"

Though I couldn't doubt that the thing was beautiful, Susana was more beautiful, and the idea of her smile after getting the necklace pushed down any desire for possessing it myself. "It'll look better on her, ma'am." I smiled. "You haven't seen my girl."

Seemingly mollified, Gran Ibo shuffled behind the counter and began to pack up the necklace in a small wooden box. I began to say something to stop her, then thought better of it. We'd have to get back to the hotel with it to put it away, so wrapping it was a good idea. "Thanks for boxing it. Lot of strange people out there tonight."

Gran Ibo said nothing, her fingers working with a dexterity a concert pianist would envy. Once it was boxed and wrapped up, she bent down and disappeared behind the counter. She popped back up, this time with a smile on her face and a small bag in her right hand. With her left hand, she beckoned me forward. As I moved toward her, she put the leather pouch on top of the box, which was wrapped in bright and colorful blue and gold paper.

"How much do I owe you for it?" I reached for my wallet, hoping she took plastic.

"What you got in your left front pocket, boy?"

My hand froze before I had my wallet out. Her voice still had that vibrant quality, but what she had said struck me as odd. I reached into the pocket she indicated and pulled out a pack of the sweet gum that was sold in seemingly every store in the south. I hadn't even had the chance to open it. I looked at the woman with a dawning suspicion and saw her smile widen.

"That look like a good trade," she said as she held out her hand. I carefully placed the pack in her hand as I took the box with my free hand.

I looked down at the pouch and shook my head and said, "I don't want this pouch, ma'am."

"You do a favor for Gran Ibo," the old woman said as she opened the pack, inhaling deeply of the gum's scent. "You do a favor for me, Keeper, and I be appreciative."

My blood ran cold as my thoughts crystalized. I tried playing dumb, which I'm especially talented at doing. "What do you mean 'Keeper', ma'am?"

"I need you give that to the Baron when you see him, Keeper." She went on like she hadn't heard my weak demurring. "He been missin that a little while."

Okay, so that pathetic denial didn't work. "I don't know who you are, but I am on vacation." My hands found the box and squeezed, my fingers squeaking on the slick paper. "I'm getting married." My voice was hard with anger and determination. "I'm not doing anyone any favors right now, so forget it."

Gran Ibo put her hands on the counter and stared back up at me. Though I was a foot and a half taller than her, I felt like the smaller one as her smoky-lensed glasses darkened. "Keeper, you say that like you got a choice."

I don't know what I was about to say in response, though it likely would have been laced with profanity. A scream from outside cut through my thoughts like a chainsaw through smoke, and it sounded like Susana. I ran towards the door, knocking over a table that had wooden stands holding ragdolls of various kinds. As they fell to the floor, I saw one with brown yarn hair wearing a t-shirt, jeans and black shoes with stars on them, its mouth open in a silent scream. It seemed to be reaching for another doll with black yarn hair that was wearing a white dress. As the second doll landed, I saw the bright red splash on the front of the dress.

Pushing the sight of the dolls out of my head, I kicked the door of the shop open onto a vision of hellish déjà vu. Susana had not been the one to scream; that was her mother. My mom was flagging down someone while Susana stood by, a look of disgust on her face. Don Salvador held his wife close, trying to shield her from the sight of someone else dying in front of them.

This time it was a woman, possibly blonde before the ruination being visited upon her, formerly porcelain skin mottling and wetly cracking in a sleeveless dress. Her left hand was against her midsection as she stumbled forward, her feet in the high-heeled shoes wobbling wildly before the ankles cracked under her weight. As she crashed to the hard road, the dead woman held out her right arm to try and break her fall. Her forearm broke away from the elbow joint and through the skin, allowing her to faceplant into the unyielding stone with a wet smack. Blood and pus from her ruined eyes and mouth flowed away from her head, but that wasn't the worst part. There was a bubbling from where her mouth should have been, and it sounded a lot like weeping.

She knew what was happening.

"Oh gods, not again." I closed my eyes on the scene, not wanting to acknowledge what was before me. My hands ached from gripping the box so tightly, and there was nothing more I wanted to do than throw it as far as I could, or perhaps to the ground and stomp on it. It might destroy the contents, it might not, but I knew it would help me feel better.

Just as I was about to do so, the woman breathed her tortured last breath, a long bubbling exhale that made me open my eyes in time to see her nearly deflate. The skin of her shoulders sagged as it seemed the muscles liquefied under the flesh. It hurt me to see it happen.

From nearby, I heard someone else scream, followed by the unmistakable sound of someone throwing up. Another unfamiliar voice shouted, "Oh fuck, man, what happened?" Immediately after that came the choked sounds of more vomiting.

Knowing what I would see before I did, I turned back to the antique store I had just exited. As expected, the door was closed and covered in "For Rent" signs, the window was dirty and dingy, looking as if it had not seen a rag in a decade, and no light coming from within. It was like I had never been in it.

Finally, to finish things up came the voice of authority, namely one of New Orleans' Finest. "Everyone stay calm." I looked to the cop and shook my head as he lied again, though unwittingly. "Everything's going to be just fine."

As I looked at the gift-wrapped box in my hands with the leather pouch on it, the faded skull grinning up at me, I knew just how false those words actually were.

Chapter Seven

"You wanna tell us what happened one more time, Mister Statford?"

The detective, Lemarchand, was only doing his job, but since he had done the same thing to me just a couple of hours prior with a different body, I was not much in the mood to answer the same questions again. Also, considering I had possibly just been shanghaied into working for one of the gods while on my godsdamned vacation, my mood likely was not the sunniest thing in the world.

"Detective, I told you exactly what happened." I kept myself from sighing in frustration only by the barest of margins. Leaning my back against a pillar, I shrugged my shoulders. "I heard screaming, I see the woman staggering forward, she falls face first into the damned road. She dies, some of the jocks over there from I Eta Pi University," I nodded towards the over-muscled guys who had stumbled onto the scene, "flip out, puke, and generally make a mess. About that time, one of your uniforms comes up, sees the corpse, calls the cavalry." I looked into Lemarchand's eyes, brown as the rest of him. "About ten minutes after that, I get the chance to meet you again so I can tell you the same story five times."

Lemarchand closed his notebook and put away his pen. He pinched the bridge of his nose like he was getting a headache, which he likely was. "Mister Statford, I know this isn't how you wanted to spend your evening, but look at it from my point of view. You're here in my city six or seven hours, and already two corpses fall right down in front of you. Wouldn't you find that at the very least somewhat odd?"

I couldn't really argue with him there. "I don't know what's going on, either, and believe me, I wish I did." I ran a hand through my hair and looked over at Susana, who was telling another detective the same story. My mom was to one side, conversing with a tall drink of water that I didn't recognize. The Don and his wife were giving a statement, with Maria looking a bit more shaken that I thought she would be, especially considering her husband's line of work. I guess there was a fundamental difference between someone with a bullet through them and being killed by what could only be considered black magic.

"You've never seen this woman before?" Lemarchand brought me back to the matter at hand.

"No, sir." I hadn't gotten a good look at the woman's face to begin with.

"Her name was Morgan Welcher," the detective said, flipping open his notebook and studying my face. When I didn't react as he thought I would, he continued. "She is, or rather was, a member of the City Council, specifically in charge of tourism. Married three times, divorced twice, widowed once. Lives over in the Garden District with three servants and a daughter."

"So what are you telling me all this for, Detective?"

Lemarchand sighed deeply. "From all accounts, the Welcher woman was rather well-liked, not just by the population of New Orleans, but by the Chief of Police." That got a light bulb to ignite above my head, which must have shown on my face. "Now you get it."

I stepped away from the pillar and said, "If I had something for you, I would tell you in a heartbeat. The problem is, I don't have anything. I'm sorry."

The cop looked deflated. "Great. Well, if you do think of anything, let me know. You still have my card?" I nodded. "Great," he repeated. "No offense, Mister Statford, but I hope we don't see each other again, at least under these circumstances."

"The same here, Detective Lemarchand." I held out my hand, which he shook. I felt sorry for the guy, as he was only doing his job, and he didn't have anywhere near all the pieces. Also, the last I checked, voodoo curses weren't covered in the manual.

Lemarchand collected his partner, a shorter and paler version of himself. The moonlight shone down and reflected off both men's heads as they left. The shorter cop nodded to Lemarchand as the taller man said something, then both took turns looking back at me before getting into their car and driving off.

Lovely; if there was a selection for "people of interest" in this case, I was on the short list.

Susana walked over a bit unsteadily, giving the spot the former Morgan Welcher had occupied in her last moments a wide berth. She had been holding it together very well, even after seeing the horror show not once but twice. My lady wrapped her arms around me and I felt her tremble. Susana was a hell of a cop, and tougher than most anyone, but this was above and beyond anything she had ever experienced. I didn't have any words for her, as much as I wished otherwise. I wished I could tell her that she'd get used to it, but I could not and would not lie to her. Even after all my years of seeing the inexplicable, I wasn't used to it.

"You okay?" I asked her, holding her close. I felt her head shake in the negative. "That's okay. Me either."

"What is going on?" Susana whispered.

"I don't know," I answered simply. "This wasn't an accident, though."

That brought a rough laugh from Susana as she looked up at me. "Oh, you think? I doubt something like what happened to her would be an accident."

I shook my head, lost in thought. "Never mind. I need to find out what those corpses are holding against their stomachs, and I need to find out why someone is having them killed so damned publicly."

Susana pushed her fear to the side as her cop-side took over. "Message killing?" She pulled away from me and stared at the place Morgan Welcher breathed her last.

"Most likely." I looked down at the box still in my hand. The pouch had gone in my left pants pocket; I vowed I would give the Baron, whoever he was, more than just the pouch when I saw him. "That or another ritual killing. We've seen those before." Susana and I both shivered at the memory of the Russian serial killer who had inadvertently brought us back together. "Plus there's the other thing."

"You mean the antique shop that hasn't been for years?" Susana went over to examine the door to the store, seeing the realtor's lock that had not been there when I walked in. "You think this is all a setup." I nodded in agreement, trying the push the anger down so I could think clearly. "But why the cloak-and-dagger? Why not just ask you?"

"Because I would have told them to kiss my ass and I'm on vacation." Closing my eyes, I tried to keep the bitterness and fury out of my voice. "I'm not a fucking puppet on a string!"

The Don broke in with a chiding tone. "*Señor*, I doubt that anyone would want to be a puppet." I opened my eyes and saw him with his hand on Susana's shoulder, a kindly smile on his face.

"That does not change the fact there are two people who died in a very dramatic fashion in front of you and," he nodded his head toward the abandoned storefront, "something very supernatural happened that I cannot explain. Something must be done."

I sighed, my head bobbing up and down in agreement. So much for staying out of things. "Okay, then, if that's how it has to be." My mind changed gears and started listing facts, of which I had few. Two people dead from a voodoo curse, one obviously affluent. The local gods had an interest in this, enough to change around time and space to open an antique shop where one did not exist. The necklace might have something to do with it, as did a leather pouch with a skull on it. I didn't discount the possibility that one or both items might be a red herring just to get me into the case. In the dictionary next to the phrase "capricious assholes" are pictures of ninety percent of the gods. In addition, it says "See also: entities who are making the Keeper miserable."

Yes, I know those are phrases and not words. I'm allowed to exaggerate a bit. Believe me: they deserve it.

"First thing we have to do is get a look at the bodies." I ran a hand through my hair as my mind raced. "They were both clutching their midsections. I don't think it was just from them being in pain. I think they were holding something to protect it." I began walking purposefully back to the hotel.

"Implying a link between the two people." Susana fell into step beside me as her father went to collect his wife.

"Something like that isn't something you do just for fun. That would be a lot of pain just for a random killing." As we walked, my mom walked toward me with a tall, dark-haired man in tow. "I imagine they're on a slab at the morgue by now with the medical examiner hoping he isn't dealing with some epidemic."

Mom spoke up. "You'd be right in that. A man named Paul Luvec is the coroner and he is keeping everyone away from the corpses until the CDC can get a look at them. That includes the police and any family members. I'm told he's rather officious."

I sighed in frustration. "So we need to figure out how to get in there without this Luvec guy getting wind of us."

Holding her hand out to the tall man, he placed three cards into my mom's hand. "Or we just walk in as three representatives of the Center for Disease Control." To the newcomer, she said, "Thank you for your promptness, Mr. Renton."

"My pleasure, Miss Statford. I'll go check on the other thing." Renton peeled off from the group, his step like a stalking lion. He was over six feet tall, tanned, and lantern-jawed. He definitely did not miss any days at the gym as evidenced by the way he filled out his suit. I got a feeling of contained menace from him, but directed towards anyone my mom pointed out as a threat. In all, I was rather glad he was on my side.

"Friend of yours, Ma?" I smiled.

"Mister Renton is one of my new people, yes. We worked together in South America last year. He's coming along nicely."

The Don perked up at that. "South America? I was given to understand you work for the government. What exactly do you do, *Señora*?"

Mom had never said much to me about what exactly she did, since at any time, she could be out of contact for days at a time, and didn't want me to worry. The whole top-secret, classified thing kind of worked with that as well. As far as the world was concerned, the agency she ran didn't exist, and she was a kind, sweet lady who went on extended absences from her non-descript office in a non-descript building in Hampton. She had three cell phones, one with more security than the President. I had never heard it ring, and she told me once that she never wanted it to ring. I didn't ask why.

That's probably why I didn't understand the significance of her response. "I'm a spirit to some, a demon to others."

Don Salvador stumbled in his steps, being caught by Maria. I thought he was going to explode. "*Eres La Espirita*?" I caught the capitalization by the Don. When Mom said nothing in response, the Don chuckled. "My thanks, then, for doing what I could not do, where I could not reach, *Señora*."

"*De nada*, Don Salvador." Mom gave me a slight shake of the head and mouthed the word "Later" when I opened my mouth. Again, I was reminded that what Mom says, goes. It did surprise me a bit that the lady had probably done more to impress Don Salvador with one sentence than I had in not only many sentences but many hours. Mentally, I shrugged. I had more important things on my plate than who was impressed and who wasn't.

Mom passed out the identification cards to Susana and me. I saw my name had been changed to Doctor Hugh, and I groaned. "Really, Ma?"

"Mr. Renton had very limited time, and did the best he could," she admonished. Susana showed me hers: Doctor Christine Chapel. I caught a look at Mom's card, and shook my head at the name Lenora McCoy.

"He's also a sci-fi geek, apparently," I chided.

"So were you, or do you not remember your Star Wars bedsheets?" She picked up the pace.

"Ma, I was five. Every five-year-old had those sheets."

"And you played with those toys until you were a teenager, and is this really the time to have this discussion?" I shut my mouth. "I thought not. Don Salvador, Mr. Renton will meet you back at the hotel. Trust that he will protect yours and mine."

"And my son?" The Don's voice was neutral.

"That is where Mr. Renton is going now, sir. He will likely be waiting for you at the hotel by now."

The Don nodded in approval. "My thanks, *La Espirita*." He moved Maria at a quicker step towards the hotel, still a quarter-mile away.

"Now, Tommy, what is your plan?" Mom looked at me.

"You're the one with the fake ID cards and mook from Central Casting, Ma." I turned the card over in my fingers as we came to a stop. "I'm still trying to pull this together."

Mom turned me toward her sharply. "Then pull it together faster," she hissed. "I come up with the plan, it involves me neutralizing a lot of innocent people whose only crime is being in the wrong place at the wrong time."

"The cards---"

"They're just to get us in so I can work. What I do is clean, surgical and leaves no witnesses, Tommy." Steel came into my mom's eyes. "If that's how you want it, that's how it goes. It will be quick. Is that what you want?"

I shook my head. "No, I don't." Taking a deep breath, I began walking for a cab that had just pulled up, dropping off a bunch of semi-drunk kids and adults. "Okay, come on."

Susana smiled at me. "You have a plan?"

"No, but I will once we get there."

As the three of us clambered into the cab, the driver turned back and looked. "Where to, pal?"

"City morgue," I said. There had to be something there, and we were going to find it.

Whether we wanted to or not.

Chapter Eight

The cab dropped us off outside the New Orleans Forensic Center on Martin Luther King Boulevard, just two miles and fifteen minutes away. Where I was expecting some huge edifice, imposing and intimidating over the neighborhood, I was rather disappointed to find a small one-story gray building with a simple black and white sign declaring it to be the New Orleans Forensic Center. Considering how many people I thought died in New Orleans under other than normal circumstances, I expected something a bit more. It was about as utilitarian a building as I had ever seen. Even the fence was a little more than standard wrought-iron, which added to the blandness of the center.

The accessory shop next door was a nice, though macabre touch.

Lights were burning in the windows, which I expected. It likely meant the coroner Paul Luvec was present, and if he was as officious as Mom said, he was working on at least one of the bodies, and had the other under guard. Pulling out my fake ID, I motioned the two ladies to follow. Usually in these situations, the best way is to get in unnoticed. Through the back door, a skylight, something. However, thanks to the lack of time and desire to keep a bunch of innocent people alive, I decided to go with the old standby.

Baffle em with bullshit.

I made my way to the front door, fixing my character in my mind. As I pressed and held the buzzer for entrance, I had a thought. Ninth, Tenth or Eleventh? Regardless, Renton and I would have to have a serious talk.

The glass door was opened by a rather harried looking lady in scrubs. Her dark skin spoke of her Creole origins, even if I hadn't heard her cussing out the buzzer I had held down. The cap on her hair was askew because of the braids she wore, which added to the sense of frazzle she emanated. The scrubs covered several necklaces with what looked like silver and wooden charms. I could smell the formaldehyde and sterilizing agents on her, although a sweeter pleasant smell was beneath it. She held the door open and looked pointedly at my finger still pushing the button for the buzzer. "Yes, the doorbell works, and may I help you?"

Playing somewhat the buffoon, an act that many would say I do almost too naturally, I pulled my finger from the button like it was hot. "Oh, dreadfully sorry." I adopted a broad Northern accent, a slightly daffy smile spreading. "Didn't know it would do all that." Whipping up my card, I showed it to her. "I'm the Doctor. From the CDC."

"Doctor who?" She looked at the laminated plastic, comparing the rather unflattering picture to the real thing. Silver earrings jangled as she moved her head from the card to my face.

"No, Doctor Hugh. That happens all the time. Sorry." I indicated Susana and Mom, who both had friendly plastic grins. "These are Doctors Chapel and McCoy. We're expected, I believe."

"Yes, not til morning, though." The woman looked dubiously at the cards. "You CDC guys are never this fast."

"Well, wouldn't you know, we were already in the neighborhood for a consult, so we got the call to check things out! Isn't that smashing?" I put my hand on the door, using slight pressure to keep it open. "Now come on, Miss---?"

"Minerva Gary. I'm the assistant coroner."

"Right, then, Doctor." I looked to my left and right, hoping both ladies still had their smiles painted on. "We won't be a moment, and I'm certain everyone will be happy to confirm there's no danger of communicability, right?" I flashed another winning smile; I'm told I can be somewhat charming when I need to be.

"Dr. Luvec won't be happy about this," Minerva demurred, but she didn't try pulling the door closed. "He's particular about his schedule, and he wanted to meet you."

In my head, I knew Mom was preparing to do some harsh and terribly painful martial arts move to get us past. I thought quickly. "Doctor Gary, we'll be happy to stop by again tomorrow morning, and we won't say a word about how you helped us tonight.

Please?" I dropped her a wink. "It's for a good cause, namely us getting out of your hair quick as we can." And keeping you alive and unharmed, I thought but didn't add.

Minerva Gary pursed her lips then came to a decision. "Okay, but be fast. Luvec's not known for being nice about anything." She opened the door wide for the three of us, ushering us inside.

The interior of the center was about what I expected from the outside: dull, dreary and utilitarian. Drab dun tile covered the floor, while the walls were a dingy white plaster. The desks were clean and clear, the computers on them nearly silent in sleep mode, the monitors dark. There were no lights on in the main office area, but the hallways were brightly lit up, glaring into my eyes. I felt such a clinical oppression from just walking in, my soul hurt. This was where dead things were, and it felt like it. This was where people were dissected to find out what ended their lives, and it was all I could do not to just push my way back out into the night air, because anything would be better than where I was.

"This way, Doctor," Minerva said, leading the three of us down a drab hallway. The doors were all that utilitarian brown-painted metal that made the place look more like a prison than a coroner's office. As we followed, the smell of antiseptic got stronger, nearly burning my nostrils. I let out an involuntary cough and began to breathe shallowly through my mouth. Minerva looked back at me and said, "Dr. Luvec doused the bodies and everything they touched with antiseptic and antibacterial fluid. He's a bit of a stickler about it."

"A stickler for what?" Susana muttered, her nose wrinkling from the strength of the smell.

"Contamination. He made sure that the cadavers were left in state, but properly decontaminated. Dr. Luvec is rather brilliant, really. Driven, though, especially after his loss."

The easiest way to keep someone talking and not thinking is just repeat the last word of the sentence they just spoke. "Loss?"

"He lost his wife in a terrible accident. I helped him as best I could, as I know what it means to lose someone you love." Minerva stopped in front of a door simply marked "Exam Room #2". "The male is in here. Dr. Luvec hasn't examined him yet as the Welcher case took precedence."

"Where's his chart?" Mom said, bringing me back to what characters we were supposed to be playing.

"Right, we'll need that, along with any effects he might have had." I put my hands in my pockets to stop the desire to cover my mouth.

"His chart is next to the examining table." The four of us walked through the doorway and the stench of alcohol hit me full in the face. I gagged slightly, trying to keep my gorge down. "I have to get back to the doctor. I was assisting him with the Welcher case."

I waved her off with a strained smile and a choked thanks. After she left, the three of us coughed for a minute or two, trying to get acclimated. I wiped the tears from my eyes and took a look at what we had to deal with.

What we had was an emaciated male corpse kneeling on the examination table. The face was down on the metal, thankfully blocking the ruined eyes and mouth from sight. From what I could see, the suit had been cut away as much as possible, though the left sleeve of the suit was still on his arm since the hand was still at his midsection. Blood and bile and pus had been wiped clear from the exposed flesh, which was pale except for the angry puckered red lines due to the slashing effect of crashing through the glass doors. The cloth around the arm was only a light pink, likely due to the amount of cleaning that had gone into making the body somewhat presentable.

Mom picked up the chart and began reading out loud. "Maurice Hickock, forty-three, Caucasian. According to his driver's license, he lived on Camp Street, which is in the Garden District, I believe. Height, five-eight, weight…" Mom whistled, "two-sixty. Whatever did this must have ravaged him terribly."

"Yeah," I said. "That body can't weigh more than a hundred." I searched for some latex gloves.

"His wallet is pretty much a lost cause," Susana reported. "It's soaked with this stuff. I can't find anything intact in it."

"Great," I muttered as I pulled on a pair of gloves. "This is going to suck." Taking a firm hold on the corpse's left arm with my left hand and bracing against the ribcage with my right, I pulled the limb steadily, doing my best not to cause any more damage than had already been done. The first inch of hidden arm was caked in reddish-brown coagulated blood, and the stench sliced through the antiseptic and into my nostrils. I gagged again and tasted bile in the back of my throat. I buried my mouth into the crook of my right arm and used my sleeve as a filter. "Gods, that's disgusting," I said, my voice muffled. I kept pulling on the arm.

"Hey *gringo*, this is interesting," Susana said, seemingly oblivious to my nearly yarking all over the place. "It seems Mr. Hickock is a land developer." When I made no comment, she continued. "At least that's what this business card says. It's about the only thing other than his license that isn't ruined."

"A developer and a councilwoman," Mom mused as she flipped through the chart. "I wonder if the two knew each other."

I had already figured they did, but had not said yet. Circumstantial evidence did not equal fact in my book, but it would be pretty godsdamned unlikely for two people who had nothing to do with each other dying in the same exact way and lived in the same neighborhood. I grunted a bit more as I pulled harder. Tendons creaked as I exposed more arm, this time up to the wrist. Even with no muscles, rigor mortis seemed to have kicked in quite well.

As Mom and Susana talked amongst themselves, I added up a few things that didn't make sense in a form of reverse-logic. Two dead people, both from high society, killed by a voodoo curse that pretty much liquefied their insides. They died the exact same way just hours apart, and in front of the same private detective who happens to be on the celestial rolodex of nearly every god and goddess that ever existed. It was likely a series of message killings, since if someone just wanted them out of the way, they would have disappeared into the bayou, never to be seen again. Whoever was doing the curse wanted everyone to know about it. That implied an agenda.

Why then, though? Curses were not, to my limited knowledge, something somebody just whipped together like a dump cake. The deaths had likely been in the works for quite a while. As I gave one last pull, I wondered just what the hell was so special about the end of April.

The hand came loose from the victim's midsection, a desiccated claw that clasped some kind of leather bag. I recognized it from Gran Ibo's shop, something she called a *gris-gris*, similar to the one in my pants pocket that had a skull emblazoned on it. The scent hit me again that I had smelled in the lobby, and I again thought of marijuana. It was a different smell than pot, though, with a sickly sweet scent that cloyed in my nose. I would check the bag out later, but at least I finally had an actual clue. It took me a moment to find a plastic bag to store the pouch in, as I had no desire to touch the rancid liquid that seemed to permeate the leather. A smile started across my face as I realized I had an actual physical clue. I know that sounds ghoulish, but I needed a break.

I quickly deflated as I realized that no matter what I found in the pouch, I did not have anywhere near enough an idea how these two bodies were connected. As much as I wished otherwise, I needed some other kind of data point, something that would link the pair of corpses together. There were pieces missing, and I needed something, anything, that told me what I needed to know.

When the door to the examination room burst open to allow a pair of orderlies to bring in a gurney with a body bag on it, I realized at that moment I needed to stop asking for things, as in anything and everything.

"Hey," one of the orderlies called out, "are you a doctor?"

Figuring I might as well go for it, I nodded. "Yeah, I'm a doctor. What have you got?"

The orderlies rolled the gurney down a ramp towards me, the wheels clattering and making a hell of a lot of noise. The load on the gurney swayed to the left and right drunkenly, with no steadying by the two men guiding the metal table. "If you're a doctor, you need to sign for this. We're supposed to pass this off to a doctor." The shorter of the two orderlies seemed to be in charge, though from their lackadaisical attitude, it was hard to tell.

I looked over at the incoming racket and froze. The bag looked almost like something was kneeled over in it, similar to both Welcher and Hickock. As the men rolled the gurney into place next to Hickock, I moved out of the way to allow them access. "Where'd you find this one?" I asked, trying to be casual.

"Far side of the Quarter, near Café du Monde," the short, barrel-shaped orderly said, utter ennui in his voice. If I didn't know any better, he might have been coming off a bomber joint or two. "Guy was utterly gross, like, his insides turned to soup. We had to actually break out the hazmat suits for this one." The nametape on his chest said "Beau".

"Thanks, Beau," I muttered, taking the proffered clipboard after setting down the plastic baggie. "What was left of him?"

"Just like the others: skin, bones and liquid puke. This guy, though, I think Felix recognized him."

I looked over at the tall skinny one who seemed to be Felix. "Who is he?"

Felix reminded me a lot of the cartoon character Shaggy, except his voice was a lot lower and quite a bit slower. Physically, though, he was a dead ringer for the green-shirted stoner. "I just said, man,

I think it's the son of that rich guy. The one with all the swampland, you know, man?"

"Oh sure, I know, Felix," I nodded sagely, scrawling a line across the paper. "Now, you and Beau here go and take the night off. You've earned it."

"Yeah, man," Felix said, his eyes drifting shut. "We earned it, man."

The two orderlies shuffled out, and I mentally cussed. A frigging land grab? That was all this was? Even Lex Luthor wouldn't do something so pedestrian anymore. This was what the Conclave thought was so damned important as to ruin my holiday? That it involved the Conclave was beyond doubt; the loa getting involved all but cinched it. That didn't answer the big question, though: Why would the various members of the local gods care about someone grabbing a bunch of real estate?

Taking a deep breath, I let the anger bleed away. A land snatch made no sense past the initial look. If it were just a grab, the son of a big-time developer would not have ended up in the morgue. If it was anything like normal, it would be some poor bastard with no power or connections laying there on the slab, and an evil local robber baron twirling his moustache in the background. This was something different. This was likely personal.

I looked over to Susana and shook my head. "You know, not many women would get to see the sights you're seeing tonight."

"Oh, yeah, *gringo*," she smirked. "This is like a dream come true. You think those guys were stoned?"

"I don't know. I don't think so, and I don't think it matters right now." I turned to the newly-occupied slab. "Let's see what this one has to say."

A new voice came from the doorway, high-pitched and nasal. "I don't think you'll find he will say very much, whoever you are."

I turned to the newcomer and got just what I expected: short, pinched features, a few strands of mousy brown hair over his pate, and a bit on the rotund side. The blue scrubs he wore fit ill on him, the shirt just a touch too long and the pants just slightly too short. Glasses were on the end of a too-sharp nose, very close to sliding off. The man oozed officiousness as he tried stalking towards me, which told me who I was about to deal with. "Dr. Luvec, I presume?" Without waiting for a reply, I launched into my spiel. "Smashing to meet you! I'm Doctor Hugh, and these are my assistants---"

"You are no more a doctor than I am the King of Mardi Gras, sir," Luvec spat with something like pure venom. "I've already notified the police, and they'll be here to collect you momentarily. I don't want to hear one more word."

"I'm sure there must be some misunderstanding. We're from the CDC, sir. Here to check the bodies for communicable diseases in case this is contagious?" When Luvec said nothing, I pulled out the identification card. "Come on, a little professional courtesy? We're on the same side here."

"I think not. The both of you are going to jail, and I'm going to make sure you stay there!"

That got my attention as I looked around. I noticed three things were missing. The pouch with the skull on it and the bagged leather pouch from the victim were gone from where I had set them. A tray was next to the body of the land developer, holding only the ruined bits of a leather wallet and its contents. There was a rather obvious empty spot in one quarter of the tray where I had put the two pouches.

The third thing missing was my mom, which explained the first two missing items. That meant one of two things would happen. The first was she was looking for some way of getting Susana and me out of this mess along with getting some information on those bags. That might do some good in the short and long run, as whoever was out there killing people like this, with black magic, was unlikely to have completely wiped any trace of themselves from the pouch. Even if it was covered in liquid human, there had to be something there to find.

The other possibility was that everyone in that building except Susana and me had about fifteen seconds to live. Mom doesn't make threats lightly and though I had never seen her in action, I had no doubts of her sincerity. It would likely be quick and thorough.

Thankfully, the sounds of sirens coming closer put paid to the second choice. Of course, it just meant that I was getting arrested with my future bride. While her father was in town. Who ran the Mexican Mafia.

Boy, do I know how to impress or what?

Chapter Nine

There is something to be said for thinking, or at least having time to think. Usually, I have to live in the moment, make snap decisions, and constantly keep moving to keep alive. No matter what the self-help crowd says, there isn't always time to think things through. Most of the time, day-to-day decisions are made spur of the moment, with barely a second taken to wonder why that decision was made in that particular way. Most people either don't know or don't care why they do things as long as they get done.

The chance to think, though, is one of those wonderful times when there is time to take a deep breath, relax, and start putting things in order in the mind. It's where I could take disparate pieces of a puzzle and join them together into some kind of sense. Point A would go to Point B, and so on, until I got an idea of who was behind whatever was going on.

Granted, I wasn't even sure what was going on, but so far it involved three dead people, and that was just in the prior twelve hours, so it couldn't have been good.

Pieces were there, though. The pieces were definitely there, even if they didn't fit perfectly. Behind my closed eyes, I drew lines connecting a land owner, a councilwoman and a real estate developer. I couldn't say for sure, but considering how each had ended up in such an odd position, kneeling forward and holding their stomachs, it followed some logic that each had held those pouches. I would have almost bet money on it.

Of course, I had no idea what was in them, but considering that not only was I in the biggest spot for voodoo in the United States, I had been visited by one of the loa, and as such had a burning hunch that the bags were the way these curses had been passed to their victims. That made me wonder why they had the bags to begin with, though.

That line of thought led to my wondering about the reason for the dead people. Yeah, I know the curse was what killed them, but that didn't answer the why. Only the truly insane do things just to watch the world burn, but considering there weren't huge crowds of corpses clutching their own little Bags O' Doom up and down Bourbon Street, that meant either someone was trying to send a message or was trying to prevent something, or possibly both. No matter what, it still didn't add up to anything useful, so I left that thread to hang.

Time to think, always a wonderful thing to have. Unfortunately, having that time while locked up in a jail cell is not usually the best way to get it. There are easier ways, I imagine.

I hadn't seen Susana since they had taken her to the women's side of the lockup, so I had been stuck in the cooler with a group of three rather fun-looking gentlemen who looked as though no matter which side of the bed they had woken up on, it would have been the wrong side. The leather jackets and denim jeans that looked as if they'd been through about fifteen bar brawls added to their menace, along with the unshaven faces and unkempt hair. When I had walked in, I had seen one of them, the largest of the trio, wiping blood from his knuckles with a handkerchief.

Which was pretty much why I had done my best to keep my mouth shut and not cause any trouble. I had enough to deal with at the moment without three of the steroid crunchy types harshing my vibe, as the kids said. As usual, though, I might as well have wished for the moon and a vacation that didn't involve voodoo curses and people dying right in front of me.

I smelled him before I heard him, though it was a near thing. Tequila, bourbon, and something else warred with blood and vomit, making sure that I knew he was close. He was about six-six and packing about two-fifty in hard muscle, and not one bit of it was nice. His hands looked the size of free weights a bodybuilder would use, and where the leather vest and t-shirt didn't cover, an intaglio of tattoos depicting horrific scenes of biblical and not-so-biblical destruction showed. The boots were the typical heavy black leather engineer boots which seemed popular with bikers, as they allowed massive damage just by virtue of their weight.

The guy towered over me, as I was sitting down on a bench, my back against the wall. I looked up at him with a blank stare, wishing not for the first time that Susana and I had just eloped. He was leaned over me, both arms bridging above my head, muscles alternately tensing and relaxing. A sandy mustache and beard completed the man's hatchet face, dark brown eyes looking down on me with predatory glee.

"Help you, friend?" I said, hoping to head things off before they got messy.

"Dat's funny," he answered, the accent painting him as an out-of-towner also, likely from New York City or thereabouts. "Wuz just about to axe you the same thing."

"No, I'm good, thanks." I closed my eyes again, though I got a good look at the guy before I did. I had one shot, but that was hopefully all I would need.

"Youse got anything ta keep me from beatin the shit outta you?" The guy's breath was so bad, I almost expected my hair to bleach out.

"No, but if I had a thing of breath mints, I'd beg you to take them all." I opened my eyes back up to slits, watching where his boots went.

I heard a couple of rough laughs from across the cell; those were his friends. They weren't interested in this other than the potential humor value.

"You think youse a wiseass, huh? You think yer funny?" He slammed a fist to either side of my head, making the stone vibrate with the impact. I didn't flinch, as I had expected it.

"He thinks he's a comedian, Harry!" One of the other guys shouted, "Maybe you should show him some manners."

"I tink I better," Harry muttered. "Yeah, I better show youse who's boss." I heard the cracking of knuckles. "Ain't nobody laughs at me! Gonna take you apart!"

He seemed to be psyching himself up to do just that, which told me something very important. The guy was a bully, and I had read somewhere and knew bullies don't want to fight.

They just want to beat you up. I wasn't about to oblige him.

Judging by the gutter smell in my face from his shouting, Harry was still bent over me, the alcohol breath blowing right into my nose. From that and seeing his boots in the bottom of my vision, I knew what had to be done. As I felt one of his hands close on my shirt, I brought up my right leg as hard as I could between his legs, the shin connecting with his vulnerable crotch. Breath exploded from him in quick blast, ending in a quiet whimper. My eyes snapped open, taking in exactly where and how I wanted to hurt this guy. With my own hands, I grabbed the lapels of his vest solidly. With a roar of my own, I pulled him face-first into the wall. The strike of his head made a solid thud, like the way a softball sounds when it gets a good hit from a bat. Harry's hand, which had tightened on my shirt after my first shot, loosened a bit, then squeezed again.

Maintaining my place on the bench, I drew both my legs in, then thrust them out to full extension as hard as I could, not caring where exactly I hit. I may not be the strongest guy in the world, but I had kept up in the gym, and running for your life definitely builds up strength in the legs. Add to that I was braced against the wall, and I had the perfect platform with which to cause some major pain. I even angled up a bit to give myself better leverage.

My heels made contact right below the sternum, which I knew would cause some severe pain and problems for Harry. My strike was true, making Harry begin to gasp and heave to try and catch his breath. Not letting go of Harry's vest, I kicked out again, this time aiming for his crotch. My heels hit squarely, bringing another gasp and whimper. Using my legs, I let go of the vest and pushed Harry back as hard as I could, sending him flying to the hard stone floor. He curled into a ball, trying to protect his injured areas.

I jumped up and started kicking him in the stomach and the chest and arms, wherever I could get a target. My anger had taken me over, anger from all the insanity that had happened in just the prior half a day. There it was, probably just past midnight, and instead of sleeping with my lady, I was stuck in a jail cell beating the shit out of a biker. I wouldn't even have been in the cell if the Conclave had just for once in their godsdamned existence let me have one week in peace. Instead, like a monkey on a string, they decided that I wasn't doing anything important and I could do whatever they wanted.

After about half a dozen kicks, the rage bled away. That, and I was just tired of kicking someone while they were down. Granted, I had been taught that if I was ever in a fight, always fight to win. Well, I had won. Huzzah. I looked over at Harry's two friends, likely with the same bland bored look and asked, "You need anything, friends?"

They both held up their empty hands to me. "No way, man. We're good."

I walked to the bars. "Good. Now get his smelly drunk ass out of my sight." I rested my arms on the bars, trying to get my emotions back under control. Usually I didn't lose it like that; I was lucky I hadn't killed him. Of course, with the booze and pot in his system, he likely wouldn't remember the ass-kicking I had just given him. A shame, really. Someone should always be able to recall when they've had their ass beaten soundly, even when drunk and---

Stoned.

Oh crap.

"Hey," I said, turning to the two guys still standing. "What did he smoke?"

"Man, you don't need to beat him up again," one of them answered. He was a touch shorter than Harry, but reed-thin. "He was just having fun."

My patience was at an all-time low, and I clenched my fists tightly. "Listen, Poindexter, stop fucking around. What did he have to smoke? Wasn't pot, was it?"

"Naw, man, he picked up some new stuff from around here."

"What is it? I'm not asking you again."

"Lay off, man. It's called mugwort. Smells like weed, but sweeter. Supposed to be good for you." He indicated the moaning and bleeding Harry. "He mixed it with regular weed. Not smart."

"Where'd he get it?"

"Some shop up on Rue Royal. Only place that has it all year round."

So that was the scent coming from the bag. I had no idea what mugwort was, nor why smoking it was supposed to be good for you, but it was New Orleans; lots of things apparently weren't what they seemed. Lots of smoke and mirrors seemed to be par for the course. I needed information and I wasn't going to get it while sitting in a jail cell taking my frustrations out on idiots. Unfortunately, I had left my Get Out Of Jail Free card in my other pants. Just my luck.

I sat back down and thought a bit more. Harry and his two Hendersons were keeping away from me, which suited me fine. My eyes slipped closed as all the events of the last few hours ran through my head. The only good thoughts I had were that Mom had gotten away and she had the bags. She'd use her super-secret agent crap and let Susana and me get back to our lives. I wanted nothing more to do with any of it.

The door at the end of the hall opened with a loud clang, jarring me from my reverie. The back of my head stayed in contact with the concrete wall, and my eyes stayed shut. Footsteps approached, and I was at the point where I honestly did not give a damn. The steps stopped outside the cell. I kept my eyes closed, because there was absolutely no way I was going to get any kind of help.

"Statford?"

Oh, come on.

"Yes, Detective Lemarchand?" I turned my head slightly to the right and opened my eyes just slightly. "What can I do for you?"

"Actually, it's what I can do for you." The dark-skinned detective jingled keys in front of me. "You're free to go." I didn't move an inch. Not even a muscle twitched as I silently regarded him. "Didn't you hear me?"

"I heard you," I allowed. "I'm just waiting for the catch."

Lemarchand looked genuinely surprised. "Why does there have to be a catch?"

My answering smile had absolutely zero humor in it. "Have you seen the kind of day I'm having?"

"Well, I do have just a couple of questions I'd like to ask before I turn you loose." Lemarchand held up his empty hand in a placating gesture. "You're getting out regardless. These are just for my own personal information."

"Fine. Is Susana Marquez free?"

"She was released about twenty minutes ago." Lemarchand took notice of the beaten and battered biker being tended to by his friends. "What happened to him?"

Without missing a beat, I answered, "He fell down some stairs. Any other questions?"

Lemarchand shrugged as if to say it wasn't his fault that the big oaf was clumsy. He pulled a small notebook from inside his coat. "Why'd you go to the forensic center?"

"It was on the tour," I deadpanned.

Lemarchand looked up at me over the notebook. "The tour?"

"Yeah, the tour. The one that started with a guy looking like an extra from *Raiders of the Lost Ark* and continued with some chick dying in front of me so messily it took a squeegee and a wet/dry vacuum to get all of her up."

For the record, I *may* have been a little bitter.

"Mr. Statford, I know none of that was your fault, but you did gain access to a secured location with false identification." Before I could speak, he held up a hushing finger. "The coroner wanted you charged with every single possible thing in the books, and a few that aren't. The only thing that would have stuck was the false IDs."

I stood up and threaded my hands through the bars, leaning on them. "'Would have'?" I repeated.

"Seems you have some friends in high places. The State Department said you and Ms. Marquez are working for them on something of national importance." In my head, I high-fived Mom, but wondered what that favor had cost her. "I'd just like to know what that is."

"Can you keep a secret?" When Lemarchand nodded, I said, "So can I. Sorry. You know how this all works." I felt a little bad lying to him, but I had other things to do. From the way his jaw clenched at my words, I took a guess. "These aren't the only three bodies, are there?"

Lemarchand narrowed his eyes in suspicion. "How'd you know?"

"Call it my amazing powers of deduction. How many?"

The cop smiled. "You answer my question, I'll answer yours." I shrugged and nodded. "So what kind of thing is it for the State Department?"

"That's what we're here to find out. We don't know much about it, so we're looking for any clues." Gods, I love being able to lie and tell the truth at the same time. "Your turn, Chuckles: How many dead?"

"Eight others, all in the same condition. Four of them over in the lower Ninth Ward, a couple in Chalmette, and two more at the marina off Paris Road." When I gave him a blank uncomprehending stare, he clarified. "That's near the bayous to the east of here. A total of eleven bodies, and I have no fucking clue why or how. Even Luvec is stumped."

"In a group or one at a time?"

Lemarchand read something in his notebook. "All at different times, though they did seem to die more than one a day." He nodded as he confirmed something. "They died within the past three weeks, since the beginning of the month, to be exact."

"Did you find anything weird on the bodies?"

"Just odds and ends," Lemarchand said as he flipped through his book. "Nothing out of the ordinary. Why?"

"I was wondering if the dead had any other things in common."
That was a bit of a red flag. The (I assumed) lead detective on
several high-profile murder cases either had no idea about the little
pouches the bodies carried, or didn't consider them important. The
only other option was he had made the evidence of the bags
disappear, which did not sit well with me. "None of them have any
connections, I take it?"

Lemarchand shook his head. "They were all locals, and mostly
had clean records. There's nothing connecting them to each other
outside some business arrangements, which were all on the level. I
checked."

"Then I can't help you from in here, Detective." I indicated the
bars.

"Right." Lemarchand unlocked the door after I removed my
hands from between the metal bars. "If you do find anything out,
let me know, please. These are my people. I swore an oath to serve
and protect them."

I nodded and passed Lemarchand as I walked out, waving to the
Three Amigos still in the cell. Harry was still out of it, which was
fine by me. I picked up my personal effects, and was happy to have
my stuff back and in one piece. It wasn't my first time getting stuff
back from the lockup, but it was the first time I had gotten a free
pass from the United States government. My tax dollars at work.

For the moment, though, I still had no idea who was behind almost a dozen dead bodies melting in front of people. I walked to the exit, looking forward to breathing free air. These people had died during the month of April, too, which made no real sense. If it was a ritual, it was like nothing I had ever heard. Even then, it wasn't like there was any big thing going on in April. I mean, there was Passover, Easter and Tax Day, but those had already passed. Something wasn't adding up.

A lot of some things weren't adding up, but as I pushed my way out into the open air of New Orleans, I sighed. Susana ran up the stairs to me and held me. I hugged her back, wishing I could just have someone else take care of this whole mess. This was what I got for being so good at my job.

No good deed goes unpunished.

Chapter Ten

Surrounded by heaven is how I woke up.

The hotel room was something out of the movies. Not the splatter-horror movie that I seemed to be in but the romantic-comedies that Susana could only get me to watch under threat of pain. I can say that I came back to consciousness deep in the covers of the softest blanket I had ever known. The mattress seemed to swallow me up and the pillows were incredible. All around me was opulence, something in which I had rarely indulged. Cream-colored walls, ivory bedclothes, filtered sunlight coming through the curtains on the window, all just making me want to crawl as far back into the land of Nod as I could as fast as I could.

All through the night, dreams had plagued me, trying to make me see things I had no desire to see. It was like my mind was no longer my own. I was being told, whether I liked it or not, I was going to find out what was turning people into bleeding Silly Putty. Being told to do something is the worst way to get me to do things, but in this case, I had very little choice. Whatever was going on in New Orleans was involving not just me, but my family. In addition, it was being about as subtle as a bazooka to the face and about as safe. That was enough to give me reason not to find seven tickets out of Louis Armstrong, headed anywhere. If it could happen here, it could happen anywhere. Like the song says: "Nowhere to run, baby."

Nowhere to run, and nowhere to hide.

A few hours of sleep, fitful though it was, did wonders for my energy levels, which had been slacking thanks to my aforementioned fear of flying not allowing me any rest alongside people dying around me and getting arrested. Even with the bad dreams, I had managed to catch enough rest to get my third wind. My second wind had been spent the night before in the jail cell, along with likely any luck I could muster over the next few days.

I pulled myself out of the cocoon of covers and swung my bare feet to the floor. Gods, I hated mornings. Checking the clock, I grunted. There were only three hours left of the morning, which meant I had to get to work. I croaked out Larry's name as I heaved myself to my feet, making a beeline for the empty cup on the dresser I was going to fill with water from the bathroom sink.

Like a shot, Larry appeared, wearing some kind of open-throated white silk shirt, khaki pants and deck shoes with no socks. Again, I marveled at how he seemed to always wear the height of fashion. His eyes raked me up and down, taking in the corkscrewed hair, the boxers, and the white t-shirt, which he apparently found rather pedestrian. "You could have waited until you were completely dressed, Thomas."

"No time, Larry," I yawned, filling the cup with cool water. The bathroom was spacious enough that my words echoed off the tile. Larry stood in the doorway as I shut off the water from the sink. "I need information, and you're going to either give it or find it. I want to wrap this up really quick and very painless."

"In other words, nothing like any other time you have had a case?"

I looked over at Larry, noting the wry smile. "Ha. Ha. It is to laugh." I took a long drink, letting the cool liquid fill me. After draining and refilling the cup, I leaned on the bathroom counter. "Mugwort."

"Excuse me?"

"The guy in the cell with me last night totally reeked of it, and I smelled something a hell of a lot like it coming from the little pouch Hickock was holding when he died. That makes it likely there was some in there. What is it?"

Larry went silent for a moment, then said, "It is a very popular root in voodoo, one designed for protection." The spirit paused, then continued. "If memory serves, when combined with a piece of High John The Conqueror root in a *grigri* bag, it is a very impressive ward against evil."

"High what?" As he was about to explain, I waved away the explanation. "Forget it. What else is it for?"

"Roman soldiers would put it in their sandals to ward against fatigue, and it has uses in the Far East in moxibustion, where it was burned on pressure points of the body, similar to acupuncture. Smoking it supposedly provides lucid dreaming and prophecy, among other things."

"So it's protection, huh?" Larry nodded. "Didn't do those folks any damned good."

"Tell me how you found the bags, Thomas." After I related the removal of the pouch from the body, Larry's eyes lit up. "You said there was another bag that you received from an old woman?" I nodded. "Gran Ibo, you said her name was?" Again, I nodded. Larry pinched the bridge of his nose with his fingers. "Oh dear."

I sighed in complete exasperation. "Larry, who is Gran Ibo?"

"We must work on your studying, Thomas." At a withering look from me to make with the explaining, Larry cleared his throat. "Gran Ibo is the swamp witch, the crone, the loa of patience and wisdom. For her to act, it must be very dire indeed." The spirit gazed at me, holding me to the spot with such mournful countenance I almost got tears in my eyes. "This is only going to get worse."

"So what do I do?"

"These pouches were leather, yes? That is rather odd." Larry silently leaned against the wall, letting me shuffle past to get back to the bedroom. "*Grigri* bags are usually made of flannel, the better soak up the whiskey they are to be soaked in every Friday."

I looked around for Susana and didn't see her. She was likely down in the bar getting more nutrition in one meal than I usually got in a week. I began pulling on a clean pair of pants and a t-shirt from the luggage. "That's all well and good, Larry, but what the nine hells does soaking flannel have to do with people looking like wax figures in a blast furnace? What about the other pouch?"

"The one with the skull?" I nodded. "Likely, it belongs to the Baron Samedi."

As I was seated on the bed putting on my shoes, I wasn't quite in the position to smack myself in the forehead. "From the Bond movie!"

"Not as blatantly evil nor as chaste, but yes." Larry paced back and forth, spouting off ideas to me at every turn. "The Baron is one of the greater *loa*, Thomas, and is one with whom to trifle. He is rather…" At that, Larry paused, seemingly searching for the right word, then decided on, "a gregarious individual."

My wallet went into my back pocket, and my room key and car keys in the front right pocket. My phone went into my left. "Horndog extraordinaire?"

"To put it exceptionally mildly, yes. He also prefers to chew tobacco and drink copious amounts of whiskey."

"And this is a 'greater *loa*'?" I pulled my phone out to check for messages. The only one was from Susana, which said to meet her in the lobby restaurant. "Sounds like one of those figurehead gods. Goes nowhere, does nothing."

Larry tutted at me quite sternly. "On the contrary, Thomas. The Baron is quite important in life and death, as in he has the power of life and death. He can give life and take it, leading those from the land of the living into the realm of the dead. He can even bring the dead back to life, should he so desire."

"Magic," I spat. "I hate magic."

"No, Thomas, not magic." Larry looked at me with disapproval before launching into the role of professor. "Magic is not real."

"Raising the dead isn't magic?"

"Not at all. What is perceived as magic is little more than the gods granting favor to certain mortals in exchange for something, be it service, blood, riches or some other prized possession. Those charlatans you see calling themselves magicians are rarely if ever given abilities by the gods. Those who call themselves illusionists are more honest."

"So someone gives the gods, say, a year of their lives to a god, and they get the power to raise the dead, for example? That's pretty cheap."

"Hardly, Thomas. There are some abilities that the gods cannot or will not grant to a mortal, and that would rank at the top of the list." Larry raised a finger and tapped his chin. "I can think of nothing that would appease a god enough to give the power of resurrection to a mortal. That would be akin to giving a child a nuclear weapon and the means to detonate it. No, Thomas, no member of the Conclave would grant that."

"How does it work? This grant, I mean?"

"A supplicant prays to the proper god in the correct way, the god decides to grant the favor or not." Larry shrugged. "Usually not. It may seem like magic, but it is by the grace of the gods, nothing more. It would be something on the order of making things disappear, superhuman strength, that sort of thing."

"Lovely," I muttered. I was dealing with clerics. "I swear I will shoot the first son of a bitch to cast magic missile at the darkness in the ass. Twice." Larry seemed unclear of the reference and I had no desire to try and explain it to him. "Anyway, Gran Ibo gave me the bag to give the Baron, I give it to him, and that takes away one job I got saddled with."

Coming to a decision, the spirit smiled. "As you seem to have something of the Baron's, I will find him and let him know. Bringing him around the women in your family could be somewhat inappropriate. I will not be long." Before I could utter a word,

Larrisimus had vanished to wherever he went to find a horndog *loa* missing a leather bag.

"Well, that was educational," I muttered, trying to get my thoughts squared away on the task at hand. Closing and locking the door, I made my way down the hall to the elevators, working my way around obviously hung over tourists who probably wanted nothing more than a Bloody Mary to take the edge of the hair of the dog that bit them. Poor bastards. Some of them smelled like they had had enough alcohol to be embalmed. Others had tried the old trick of dousing themselves with aftershave, because that always never worked.

The lobby was rather deserted, which suited me just fine, as was the restaurant. In fact, only my mom and my potentially extended family were seated there. They were wolfing down, at least from the smell, eggs, bacon, sausage, toast, coffee by the gallon. Though it did stir my hunger, I forced down my desire to dive in by just grabbing a glass of orange juice. Food would have to wait; the thought of liquid people still sat in my mind.

"You are up, Thomas!" The Don seemed in high spirits, especially considering I had gotten his daughter arrested the night before. "It is about time."

I sat next to Susana, and took a deep pull on the juice. It was either fresh-squeezed or stuffed full of magic because I felt my energy levels go through the roof. "Good morning, sir. I needed the extra sleep, and I needed to talk to my informant."

Don Salvador leaned forward conspiratorially, a look somewhat ruined by the smile on his face. "You have an informant here? You are better connected than I had been led to believe."

"Papa!" Susana gave him an arch look. "You've been spying on him?"

"Of course he has!" Maria dabbed the corners of her mouth with a napkin. "I told him to do so, *mija*."

Susana let out an exasperated sigh. "You're both terrible!" She rolled her eyes and looked at me. "So what did Larry say?"

"He has no real idea, except the guy one of those bags belongs to is a big time *loa*." When no one reacted, I clarified. "A pretty big boss-man in the local underworld, so to speak. Anyway, I figure once I get the pouch to him, this should all be over and we can go back to our regularly scheduled happy time."

"What about the bodies?"

"I figure that's a problem for the local PD. I have absolutely zero interest in getting involved here."

Mom spoke up then. "And if you must get involved?"

I smiled grimly. "Then someone is going to really wish they hadn't messed up my plans." I grabbed a plate and began to shovel food onto it in preparation to transfer it in copious amounts to my piehole. "I don't see why I'd have to get involved, though. That stuff is magic, and not the kind of weirdness I get involved with."

As I sat down next to Susana, who was daintily sopping up egg with a piece of toast, Paolo spoke up. "This 'weirdness' you speak of, *señor*, what is it?" He glanced at his sister, who was carefully appearing to not pay attention. "Susana, she has told of some strange things that are difficult to believe. How much of it is true?"

Looking over at the love of my life, I raised an eyebrow. "You told the family about me?"

"It's not like they wanted to hear about my job," she retorted.

"I'm flattered, and I don't know what she's told you about what I've done---"

"Everything," she interrupted.

That made my mouth drop. "Everything?"

"From the Godslayer to the Master of Assassins to fire gods raining hell and damnation upon the Hampton Roads area." Susana rattled off the events in our lives with an almost mechanical precision. "I left a few things out from around the Godslayer, but other than that, they know it all."

Smiling, I said, "You left out the part about knocking me the hell out in an interrogation room?"

Don Salvador spoke up. "No, Thomas. She described that moment in rather concise detail."

I gave Susana a baleful eye. "Of course she did." I took another drink of my juice and refilled it from the carafe. "In that case, it's all true. Every single bit of it."

"You work for God?"

"Gods. Plural. I am the lucky, or unlucky, depending on your point of view, bastard who works as a go-between with gods, their lieutenants, and mortals. It's a dirty job, and I'm the sucker who has to do it."

"Forgive me, but that is very hard to believe," Maria said after sipping at her coffee. "How is there more than one god?"

I shrugged. "The gods didn't begin when the Council of Nicea put all the books of the New Testament together, nor when Pangu hatched an egg. It's not even a case of *ex nihilo*, or 'from nothing'. The gods spring up and are eternal, sometimes waning but never not being gods. I can't explain where they come from. I can only say that they are up there," I pointed at the sky, "down there," I pointed to the ground, "or wherever they particularly want to be at any given time."

"These gods," Don Salvador said slowly. "You... *work* for them?" I nodded. "How do they pay you?"

"Cash, usually, though I take plastic or even a check, as long as it's certified." At the skeptical look on his face and the bemused look on Susana's, I said defensively, "Hey, my landlord doesn't take favors from deities, just cash on the barrelhead." I took another bite of crisp bacon, bad for my arteries but good for taste. "I gotta make a living somehow."

"So this informant, does he work with the gods as well?"

"In a way. He's a go-between for me and the gods, you could say." I drank the last of my juice and looked at Mom. "You know where we have to go?"

"Mr. Renton was able to identify the contents of one of the pouches." She pulled a piece of paper with clear precise writing on it from her purse. "The other would not open, and he was loathe to try anything more invasive than just pulling the drawstring."

"The one with the skull on it?" When she nodded, I let out a snort of disgust. "Yeah, that one's the Baron's. I doubt anyone on this side of the weirdness can open it. What did you find?"

She looked down the list. "One mushroom top containing large amounts of psilocybin, camphor, Ipomoea jalapa, or High John the Conqueror root, powdered jellyfish, an etching of Jesus in ivory, a small doll, a lock of hair---"

"And mugwort," I blurted.

"Yes, and mugwort. I've done some checking and this is the standard contents of what's popularly called a mojo bag." I was about to say something but Mom interrupted me. "This would be a proper mojo bag with one exception." When I shut my mouth, she said, "It has the wrong number of objects in it. From what I understand, that would make its abilities as a protective item useless."

I shook my head. "So whoever got these bags to the victims knew they were worthless and wouldn't stop any kind of curse they laid on them. Meanwhile, the victims think they're all hunky-dory and protected from all the evil magic in the world."

"But why would they all have the same bags?" Susana asked. "What do they have in common?"

"Three of them have to do with government and land," Mom said. "It would stand to reason that the others had something to do with property development as well."

I sighed. "There has to be more to this than just a ridiculous landgrab. No one is stupid or petty enough to kill nearly a dozen people just to get their hands on some acreage. It's just too small a deal."

From my left came Larry's voice, startling me. "Perhaps this will make it a larger deal, Thomas." I stood up and looked at Larry, likely appearing like a loon staring at thin air.

I completed the appearance of a crazy person by talking. "What did you find?"

"It is what I did not find. The Baron Samedi is missing, and is presumed captured."

I sat back down suddenly, my breath exploding out of me. A loa. Missing and presumed captured. "Yeah," I wheezed, "that would make it a big deal."

Larry persisted. "I do not think you understand. The Baron Samedi has dominion over life and death. He grants or refuses either at his whim. Those who follow him and die can only pass on with his blessing and escort to the Land Beyond."

My mind was apparently mush. "So what?"

"There have been deaths by members of the voodoo faith since the Baron went missing. If that is the case, who is allowing these people to pass over?"

Realization hit me like a bullet between the eyes. If Baron Samedi was no longer around, then someone else had his power, likely the one who was killing all these people. It meant that someone had somehow not only stolen the power of a god, but had gotten the god out of the way to keep him from taking back that power. For such an illogical situation, it was the most logical explanation, which led to me leaning on the table, holding my head in my hands.

"Oh, yeah, that isn't good," I muttered. "That isn't good at all."

Chapter Eleven

Bourbon Street is one of the most binary places in the world depending on the time of day. When the sun is up, there are a few tourists here and there, rifling through the shops for a memento of their time in the Big Easy. Most would go home with authentic plastic voodoo dolls made in Taiwan, others would bring home beads that they said they had earned flashing the crowd when all they did was hand over five bucks for a bundle of the cheap decorations. Quite a few would be nursing horrendous hangovers, staggering from one semi-open bar to another looking for the hair of the dog. Those were the folks with new tattoos they didn't remember getting, the ones missing wallets or at least most of the contents, and the ones who don't know exactly what they did but know that the handcuffs were definitely not their idea of a good time.

Of course, then there were the ones who don't remember anything, but feel violated, as if something happened in the night, something so terrible, that their mind refused to entertain the possibility of letting the memory come to the surface. Considering the last twenty-four hours, I would likely be wishing for some liquid amnesia by the time this was all over.

Mom, Susana and her family were going to split duties between checking a few things out and helping my sister and Arthur keep the kids safe. I had seen Jennifer unleash the fury once or twice while we were growing up, so I had no worries about what would happen if some yutz decided to mess with the kids. Seriously, it's like crossing a bear and a piranha with an ill-tempered sea bass. That would be certain doom to anyone stupid enough to try something.

That Susana wanted to stay behind with her family was a bit surprising, but I figured she just wanted to try and mend some fences with the old man. While he may still drive her nuts, he was still her father, and she was getting married, so it just made sense. I had never really thought how it was to just uproot and go across the country just to make a life where the family had no bearing on life. It put things into perspective for me in a way it hadn't before regarding her, and showed just how strong this woman truly was. What she saw in me, I have no idea, but hey, I try not to look gift horses in the mouth too often.

Larry had gone off to look for the Baron again, or at least some sign of him. He told me that such an action as making a loa disappear was impossible, that the rituals involved were ridiculously difficult and totally unusable by the rank and file mortal. When I brought up the possibility of another loa doing it, Larry scoffed, telling me that to do so would cause a war the likes humankind had never seen. There was no real trail for him to follow, but there was the likelihood one of the other loa knew what had happened. That was the best I was going to get on the spiritual side, and kept Larry busy.

That left me walking the streets with Mister Renton, his name just about all I knew about him. With all the errands my mom had had him doing overnight, he didn't seem all that put out and in fact seemed wide awake. He was taller than me, so he had to shorten his stride as we made our way to the next herbalist store. Renton had dark hair so black it was almost blue, cut in a more executive than military manner. Now that I got a closer look at him, the guy reminded me of a more muscular Pierce Brosnan, but without the accent and the squinting eyes. He would glance at me from time to time as we walked, which was kind of odd.

Not as odd as the fact he was wearing a full suit in the warm weather, but still, it was odd.

After the tenth look, I stopped walking. Like clockwork, he stopped as well. I turned to him and asked, "Okay, what is it?"

"What's what?" The guy had the deep commanding voice down pretty well. No wonder he was my mom's protégé.

"You've been giving me the hairy eyeball since we left the hotel, and you've been walking in step with me for a quarter-mile." I began walking again, stepping off with my right foot, and sure enough, so did Renton. "You've said nothing to me at all, and while I trust my mother's opinion and judgment of people, I haven't exactly had the most normal day."

Renton slowed slightly. "You want to know who I am." It wasn't a question.

"I think I deserve to know who and what you are," I retorted. "I need to make sure I don't have to put eyes in the back of my head."

"You don't have to, Mr. Statford." Renton unbuttoned his coat, which likely meant he had a weapon in there. More likely, he had several. "I was given an assignment by your mother and I don't plan on botching it."

"What's the assignment?"

A flicker of a smile crossed his lips. "Need-to-know. We're here."

I was about to protest when I saw that Renton was correct. We had arrived at the Sticks and Stones herbal shop, about fifteen steps from the Café du Monde which was probably the most famous sidewalk café in the United States. Looking at Renton in disgust since I imagined he had timed the arrival just right to not answer any more questions, I turned away from him and his smug face. I was starting to get tired of people manipulating me to play according to their wishes.

Of course I knew he was right to ride herd on me. My home turf was a thousand miles away; I had no real idea where I was going and what I was doing. Renton was the one doing me the favor, and if Mom said he was trustworthy, then it might be a good idea for me to lose the attitude and appreciate the backup.

I took a deep breath to bring myself to center, and to remind myself where we were. The Sticks and Stones was the fourth place we had gone that had the herbs in the recovered bag. Though usually only found in specialty shops in the rest of the country, apparently every store in the French Quarter was a specialty shop. I mentally chided myself; searching for these particular herbs in New Orleans, the voodoo capital of America, was like searching for tacos in Texas. We were not just looking for the herbs, but someone buying them in enough quantity to make the bags in this particular configuration.

I had been a little heartened by two of the other stores pointing us in the direction of the Sticks and Stones. The other store owners had told me they had no real access to the kinds of mushrooms I was talking about, and they were adamant that they never would. The said someone named Rex had everything I would need, and he ran the Sticks and Stones. By everything, they had confided semi-conspiratorially, they even meant the mushrooms. Psilocybin, or magic mushrooms, were not something sold at the local pharmacy, and required a bit of knowledge to cultivate without getting the law involved. I had never partaken, though I was assured it was not dangerous.

I was also assured that family vacations are always great fun for everyone. You can see where my cynicism comes from.

The bell on the door was a nice touch, not the usual electronic chirp, but an actual silver bell announcing our entrance. I took a quick look around, fixing the locations of various tables and display cases in my mind. There were several surfaces that had the usual tourist trappings of voodoo dolls, good luck charms, and promises of male enhancement on them. Farther in, I noted the items looked a bit rougher, less refined. There was also a mustiness to the interior of the store, earthy and peaty. The light was low, but not low enough for me to see the long-haired store owner watching both Renton and me with feigned disinterest.

He rested he head on his left hand while his right stayed below the counter. The hair was thick dreadlocks, his palm buried in the locks which hung below the elbow. Dark skin, leathery with age, shone mellow in the dim light, with brownish-black eyes following our movements. He was built pretty solidly, the tank-top he wore showing off his physique. It made me doubt he spent all his time behind the counter. He seemed about to speak, thought better of it, then decided to talk anyway.

"Help you?" The words were said with that polite disinterest that stopped just short of his eyes. A lilt of a bayou accent twisted in the question.

"Yes, I hope so." I pulled out the list of herbs from my pocket. As I did so, the shopkeeper relaxed slightly. "I'm looking for a couple of things for a mojo bag."

"An wha' bring you heah, sir?" His right hand came up from behind the counter and he straightened up. "Dere be many place roun heah that have wha' you need."

I smiled, trying to be charming. "Are you Rex? I was told you were the best and would have what I needed."

"Tha' depen' on wha' you need."

"High John the Conqueror root, mushrooms, a wax doll, and mugwort."

Rex perked up when I mentioned the wax doll. "Tha' not all you need. You need a bag, too."

"I already have one. It's for protection." I felt Renton separate from me and going left, seemingly to look at something on the wall that caught his interest.

"I don deal in mushroom. It not legal."

"Really? That's a damned shame." I did my best to look crestfallen. "Well, what about the mugwort?"

"I don have tha' either."

That got me wondering, and by "wondering", I mean "setting off my bullshit detector." I could see what seemed to be hundreds of packets of various sizes, and even in the dim light, I saw quite a few with the word "mugwort" on them. That he was willing to lie to me about something like that told me I was likely in the right place. "Hey, I just need some special stuff for a mojo bag, man," I said, edging a bit to my right, keeping my stance casual but watchful. "It looks like you got what I need right there."

"I go' nuttin, man," he answered, his eyes now skewering me with anger, "an if you keep fuckin askin, I'll bounce yer ass out the door."

I held up my hands in a placating gesture. "Hey, man, no need to get hostile!" I saw movement from the corner of my eye and did my best to ignore it. "Just here on vacation. Looking for something for the little lady. I was told you were the best for magic mushrooms and herbs and little wax dolls."

Rex sniffed at me, managing to insult and dismiss me all in one gesture. "You don know wha the fuck you talkin bout, man. People talkin like dey got something to say. You ain got no juice here. Piss off."

At that point, I figured playing the clueless tourist was about as useful as, well, a clueless tourist so I dropped the act. "Okay, Rex, how about this: tell me about the melty people and the cursed bags and I'll do what I can to make sure you don't get fingered for it in this world or the next."

That seemed to strike a nerve. His lip quivered in rage as he sneered at me. "I ain' go' nuttin fo you, now get the fuck outta my store!"

More movement to ignore. I kept my voice cool and even. "Last chance. The folks I work for aren't as nice as I am."

Rex made his move, eyes wide with both anger and likely fear. His right hand went behind the counter again, this time quickly. He was pretty fast; even with my eyes, he was very swift, and I likely would have had trouble beating him to the draw if I had a gun. Up came a double-barreled shotgun, sawn off to within a frog's hair of illegal. Both hammers were pulled back and I was facing something that, at the distance I was, would turn me into ground chuck. He raised the shotgun in my direction, the barrels shaking violently. He was either scared to death of whatever I had reminded him of, or this was his first time about to try and kill someone.

Operative word: "try".

In a move I needed to slow down in my head after the fact, I saw Renton slide in low on Rex's right like a snake. He came up with his right hand gripping the barrels of the shotgun and his left hand grasping Rex's wrist. I heard a sickening snap as Renton's fingers dug in between the tendons and separated the bones. Rex had no time to scream as his hand jerked open, allowing Renton to pull the shotgun away with ease. Keeping an iron grip on Rex's now-useless wrist, Renton slammed the man's face down on the wooden counter, a resounding thud filling the store.

They stood there a moment, Renton barely breathing heavily, the shotgun held by the barrels, and Rex, high-pitched whining coming from his throat, snuffling snot and blood, his right arm raised high above and behind his back. Whenever Rex tried to move, Renton just raised his arm a tiny bit, bringing a yelp of pain.

"That was definitely the wrong answer, Rex," Renton said, smiling. No humor was in that gesture; it was like the smile of a lizard. "In fact, there is no other answer you could have given that would have been as incorrect." Renton looked at me, eyes flat. He wasn't enjoying this, but I knew he would do anything and everything it took to get Rex to sing. Renton set the shotgun down on the counter, well away from Rex's questing hand. "Ask him what you will. He'll answer."

I went to the shop door, flipped the sign showing the place closed and twisted the lock. Feeling a little sickened, I approached. I don't approve of torture as a general rule, but the guy had been trying to vaporize me. I wasn't taking pleasure from this at all, but I had to do what I could, and Rex had the magic stuff. I leaned down until I was able to make eye contact. Our brown eyes met and I understood that Rex likely was not long for New Orleans. He was going to get the hell out as soon as he could. That meant something had him completely spooked. If it was still scaring the shit out of him even with a broken wrist and a trained killer about to pop his arm out of socket, then this was pretty bad.

"Rex, I know you provided the stuff for the bags." I kept my voice calm, making sure I maintained eye contact. "I also know you know who picks the stuff up. Tell me who, and he'll let you go."

The dreadlocks shook in the negative. "Dey kill me an mine! I say one ting, dey kill ev'rybody!"

"Who?" Renton said as he raised Rex's arm, bringing a fresh cry of pain. "Who will kill them?"

"I don know!" Rex screamed as Renton twisted the arm as he raised it. The pop was audible. I didn't think it was the shoulder popping out yet, but it was getting close. "I swea' I don know!"

I gestured for Renton to relax a bit. "How do they get the stuff?"

"I leave it out, dey take it an leave de money. I neva see nuttin!"

"What else did they buy?"

"Dey buy all good stuff, bu it make no sense!"

"What else?" When Rex didn't answer, I nodded to Renton, who lifted Rex's arm higher than before. The man screamed again so hard I thought his voice had broken. "What else!"

"Dey buy salt, beeswax candles, frankincense, honeysuckle, vetivert, an' bergamot!" Catching his breath, he continued, his voice failing him. "Dey get licorice and calamus root, too! It make no sense!"

"Why not?

"Dat stuff for bendin th' will o' someone, but th' mount dey buy, like dey gonna ben th' loa! Ain't nobody crazy enough to do dat!"

That brought a major lightbulb, and actually made sense to me. "You'd be surprised, Rex. What else?"

"Dey got a list, man!" With his free hand, Rex pointed out the register. "Dat's all I know, I swear by Papa Legba!"

I went to the cash register, an old time metal one that didn't have a bit of electronics in it. There was a folded slip of paper next to it and I picked it up. I glanced at it, then at Rex. "You're serious." My tone was flat, and Renton would have taken it as a signal to begin trying to pull Rex's arm off if I hadn't shaken my head. "What is all this for?"

This time, Rex looked at me with veiled disgust, even though the pain had to be horrendous. "Dat th' wash fo th' dead. It's used to clean the way and the tools for dat dark magic."

Renton looked at me in guarded disbelief. "He telling the truth?"

I nodded, putting the list back where I had found it. "Rex, I think it's best if you leave town. Bad things are happening, and you don't need to be involved in it anymore." I gave Renton the signal to release the wounded man. Rex cradled his arm against his chest in an eerie mirror of the people I had already seen die in front of me.

"Dat don' matter," he muttered, the dreads hanging in his face. "Dat don' matter at all. Dey know I talk to you." He began weeping. "Dey already kill mine, now dey kill me."

"They aren't going to kill you, Rex," I soothed, walking around the back of the counter where he was. My mind was racing with everything that I had learned. What I knew wasn't the whole picture, but quite a few pieces had been filled in. Things were starting to make a bit more sense to me.

"You don' get it," Rex cried, tears rolling down his face. "Dey got what dey want. Dis stuff only to make sure dey let mine go on th' otha side!" He threw his locks back, utter agony in his face. "Dey gonna make us some of dem."

Renton shook his head as he went into the back room. I gazed at Rex in pity. Whoever had done this to him had really screwed him up. "Some of what?" When Rex didn't answer, I leaned forward on the counter and shouted. "What the hell is going on?"

Rex's answer chilled me. "We be death, man. We come for you." He sighed, the sound a whisper from a grave. "Only one way outta dis."

Before I could react, he grabbed the shotgun from where Renton had laid it down. Though using his left hand, he manipulated it well enough to shove the barrel under his chin and squeeze the triggers.

In the enclosed space, the twin blasts were devastating. Muzzle flash sent stars through my eyes. The sound boomed through my ears, sending me to the floor instantly in pain. A high-pitched tone started, like a very high C-note. I covered my ears with my hands, which was like barring the door after some idiot set the barn on fire. My eyes were tightly shut, though I could still see the effects of the shotgun shells on Rex's skull from the instant before I fell. I had seen the like before, but I had been expecting it, and that time the bastard deserved it. Not so with Rex.

I felt a hand lay on my arm, and I gripped it. The hand squeezed gently, seeming to try and give some comfort. I opened my eyes and looked at the owner of the hand, or more specifically, the mangled mass of flesh and brain and bone that had been Rex's head. Weaker and weaker pulses of blood spurted from the wound, with pinkish brain matter and bright white jagged skull showing the devastation in all-too-clear detail. He had fallen right next to me by pure chance, his hand landing on me, the squeeze nothing more than nerves firing their last after such catastrophic damage. I shoved the hand away and rolled onto my stomach, pushing myself as far away from the body as possible.

Renton came in like an avenging angel, a very businesslike piston in his hand. His mouth moved but all I could hear was the tone. It was tinnitus for sure, and that was a frequency my ears would never hear again. I shook my head and covered my ears. He stopped talking and took in the scene in one quick sweep. With his empty left hand, he pointed at the headless body, then mimed shooting himself under the chin. I nodded at the pantomime and stood up, even though my equilibrium was off.

As I looked down on the body, I was flabbergasted. Something scared him enough to take such a drastic action of killing himself in the most destructive way possible. I shuddered at the thought, trying to bring myself into focus. It wasn't easy at all.

When Renton touched my shoulder, I let out a small scream, so lost in my thoughts. The good news was I heard myself, so I wasn't completely deaf. The bad news was we had another dead body, this time from definite suicide, and there I was, right at the scene of the crime.

Raising his voice to be heard, Renton said, "We need to get this cleaned up." He put his weapon away.

Pulling myself back to reality, I replied, "Why? Whoever is going to pick the stuff up is going to notice the mess."

"Lower your voice." Renton reached into his pocket and pulled out his phone. "I'll handle it. Just help me get the corpse into the back room until help arrives."

I was aghast. "You're calling a cleaning crew?"

Exhaling heavily, Renton said, "Perhaps you're right. It's not like anyone would notice the brain tissue still sticking to the ceiling." He pointed upwards. "Or the blood all over the little flannel pouches. Or the fact that Rex's eyeballs are approximately fifteen feet from each other on different tables and looking at each other." Renton indicated each location.

"Fine, then, call them." I looked at the pickup time scrawled on the list. "We've got three hours."

"It will be done in ninety minutes." Renton began to dial again, then looked at me. "Inform Mrs. Statford that we are all right, and what your plans are."

I nodded, pulling out my own phone. I dialed Mom, who seemed less than pleased to hear from me.

She had to raise her voice so I could hear her. "Why isn't Mr. Renton contacting me?"

"He's scheduling a cleanup, Ma." I sketched the encounter, which took long enough for there to be a knock on the shop door. Renton walked around me and opened it, allowing eight men in coveralls to enter. "They're here."

"Good. You have a plan, then?"

"Yeah. Stakeout. We know when someone's picking up a shipment of herbs and spices, so we're just going to sit and wait for them." I did my best to get out of everyone's way, which was easier said than done. "Did you find anything?"

"Yes, it appears that the victims do have a connection."

Something tripped in my brain. "They're all members of the same voodoo coven."

The disappointment at being scooped was evident in Mom's tone. "How did you know?"

"The numbers add up, along with all the ritual and crap." I rubbed the bridge of my nose with my fingers, the tension headache starting to add to the pain of the ringing in my ears. "Plus, at this point, it's the only wild-ass guess that makes any portion of sense. What I don't know is what binds them together." Pacing back and forth on the far side of the store, as far away from the carnage as I could be, I started brainstorming on the line. "Nothing happens without a reason. There's always something that brings a group of people together, for whatever they're trying to do."

"I've checked their histories going back five years," Mom said. "Other than this 'coven', or whatever they call it, they have nothing in common."

"There's gotta be something there, Ma." I picked up the note again, looking past the list of patchouli and olive oil and other odds and ends that sounded like the world's most disgusting salad, wondering what the hell all of it was for. "Something has to link them."

"Tommy, I get the sense that there is a deadline here, and it is fast approaching." Mom could have a dry sense of humor.

"I don't know, maybe." I walked outside, making sure the closed sign stayed as it was. The air, though not sweet, was at least clear of the cleaning chemicals the crew was using. I leaned my head against a nearby pillar, my arm between my forehead and the wood. I closed my eyes to try and see connections that just were not there. "It just doesn't make any godsdamned sense. Why now? Why the hell is all this happening now? Why to these people?"

Mom was silent for a moment, then, "I don't know."

That brought a pained laugh out of me. "You have no idea how scary those words are coming from you." I took another deep breath and let it out.

"You may think I know everything, Tommy, but I don't. I wish I did."

Silence came between us, the phone in my hand impassive to a sudden squeezing out of frustration. Bringing it under control took almost all of my energy, but it worked if only barely. I lifted my head and looked across Bourbon Street, my eyes happening upon a store garishly decorated in neon and Christmas lights. A huge poster dominated the window, showing a jar and a wispy skull coming out of broken mouth of the container. It was garishly colored, designed to draw attention from anyone not legally blind with its likely glow in the dark white paint, the dripping red letters spelling out words that became suddenly very interesting to me. "I'll call you back, Ma." My phone went into my pocket.

I began walking across the street in a daze, a couple of cars honking at me in annoyance. Ignoring them was simple, as I was focused on the brightly colored picture. To be exact, I was looking at the date on the poster. It looked very familiar.

Namely that it was today's date, April 29th.

When I got to the other side, I could read the words on the poster clearly, even though I couldn't understand them. *Casse canarie*. Great, it was either regular French or Creole French. The words were gibberish to me, so I called over a passerby. She looked about nineteen going on thirty, dressed in some kind of outfit that could charitably be called rags. Her dusky skin had been artificially paled with powder and greasepaint. I figured her for a local as she wasn't gawking at everything. In addition, she had the bemused look of a local when I beckoned her over.

"Excuse me, miss." I alternated between her and the poster, and I could feel my head starting to pound from the sense of an oncoming freight train right into my skull.

"Whatcha need, honey?" Gods, I was likely twice as old as this kid and she was calling me honey.

"What does that mean?" I pointed to the words. "My French is rusty to the point of non-existence." I tried a smile but failed.

The rictus of a grin on my face seemed to have no effect on her as she answered simply, "*Casse canarie*. It means breaking the jugs." Seeing my lack of reaction, she apparently took pity on me. "It's something the voodoo people do this time of year. They break the jugs to release the souls from purgatory, or something like that. Tomorrow is *mange-les-mortes*. The day of feeding the dead. It's a really great party. Anything else you need to know?" When I numbly shook my head, she flounced off without another word, likely wondering why some crazy tourist wanted to know about a voodoo holiday.

Releasing the souls from purgatory. Gods, this was looking worse and worse.

Chapter Twelve

There were times when I wished I could cuss effectively in different languages. Not any of the Romantic languages like French or Spanish, but the forceful, powerful words from Russia or Germany that can be considered weapons-grade by the Geneva Conventions. I wanted to be able to shout words that would cause bruising and send people to the hospital. The Germans have a word for damned near anything. There is actually a word in German for someone whose face makes you want to punch them. I swear I'm not making that up. Gods knew I had plenty of those.

However, since my lingual skills were limited in scope, I settled for muttering "Fuck!" and "Son of a bitch!" in more creative and intricate ways for several minutes as I began to piece together exactly how the Conclave had gotten me here. The bastards knew this was going to happen. They knew and they didn't care that I was going to be busy. The gods had decided that my happiness didn't matter at all, and I needed to be where they wanted me. That I was on vacation with family did not seem to affect them one little bit. Hell, it likely gave them a big celestial woody as they knew I would fight harder to protect my loved ones.

I don't mind being given a job, but when I'm suckered into something, or when someone lies to me to get me to do something, I get a little touchy.

"Tom, what is it?" Renton came up behind me. I had no idea how long I had been standing there, but the shadows had lengthened. I could see him in the reflection of the window holding the poster. He approached warily, as I did not seem to be all that happy. That he was right did nothing for my sense of self.

"The fuckers set me up." I bit off each word like it was poison. "They got me down here to do this job for them."

Renton raised his eyebrows. "I'm afraid I don't understand."

"It never is enough for them. They set this all up so I could be here to find out who kidnapped one of their own, and they could have hired me weeks ago to do it." I moved to the wooden pillar holding up the second floor of the shop. My fist struck the wood, sending a shock up my arm and making me hiss. "The bastards couldn't have just been up front and honest and said they had a job." I hit the pillar again, relishing the pain. "Like a fucking monkey on a godsdamned string."

"If this is about the deities you supposedly work with, Tom, that is not important right now." Renton looked at me impassively. "The crew is done, and no one will be the wiser. You said something about a stakeout?"

"Yeah, why not?" I stalked back across the street to the Sticks and Stones, ignoring the blaring horns of passing cars. Entering the shop was like déjà vu, all over again, only this time, there was no one behind the counter. The place smelled exactly like it had the moment Renton and I had walked in, down to the stench of patchouli. There wasn't even any cordite in the air, and there is a ton of gunpowder in two shotgun shells. That there was a cleaning crew in town made me glad that Mom had let me handle things at the morgue, as they would have gotten plenty of use the night before.

I picked up the list and scanned it again. At the bottom of the page were five words I had missed before, which chilled me to the bone. The writing of the ingredients was neat and precise; the pencil marks were light but sharp enough to cut glass. Whoever wrote the little benediction at the bottom apparently knew they had terrible penmanship and had written it like a third-grader-turned-serial-killer. The heavy strokes were thick and deep, almost like a marker had been used.

"Last time pays for all," the note said. "Oh yeah, not ominous at all. Hallmark could make a mint off that well-wish! Fuck." "Whoever wants all this crap will be by soon," I said, surveying things with a critical eye. Damn, those guys did excellent work. "We stake the place out, tail the bad guy, find the Baron and I'm done. Piece of cake."

Renton put a hand on my shoulder and squeezed to get my attention. I turned to face him. "Anger has no place here, Tom. We think carefully, act appropriately, and strike clearly."

I pulled away. "You have no idea what it's like to be a puppet."

The taller man smiled and got a faraway look in his eye. "You'd be surprised, Tom. I didn't always work for your mother, and we didn't always agree."

"That sounds familiar." I chuckled ruefully.

"I know," Renton said simply. "It doesn't feel good being forced to do the right thing, even when you want to do it."

I shook my head in resignation. "Did I mention I hate being preached to?"

"No more than I do. Your mother, however, can be very persuasive."

"That she is. The crew has everything in place?"

Renton nodded. "They have the shipment of whatever was on that list ready to go. Whoever he is has some strange ideas about shopping."

We left the store to head across the street, this time watching where we were going and not pissing off anyone driving. As we settled into the Café du Monde and ordered a pair of coffees and a double-serving of beignets, I mused at Renton's stoicism. He reminded me of the stories of the Roman centurions who had no problem coming up with straightforward solutions to whatever issues they faced. All that mattered to him was fixing the problem, regardless of what had to happen to himself. I understood it all too well, and if my mom had designated Renton her protégé, that meant he understood it as well. We sat drinking our coffee, a strong brew, in a companionable silence as rainless clouds rolled in, bringing a bone-deep chill.

We were well into our second cup when I got a rather abrupt and rude surprise.

Renton smiled slightly, his eyes cutting to the right where the shop was. We had positioned ourselves that both of us would be able to see the door to the Sticks and Stones, with me looking east and Renton watching the west. Foot traffic had picked up a bit, and cars were less frequent. Even with the increase in pedestrians, it was difficult to miss who Renton had zeroed in on. I could see her, and my brain did a backflip and a double-take.

Minerva Gray, the assistant coroner, was walking out of the Sticks and Stones with the goods. Two large canvas sacks worth of pseudo-mystical odds and ends didn't seem to weigh her down at all. She was wearing a tan raincoat, as if in preparation for bad weather. From where I sat, I could see the determination set in her face and wondered how I had missed it before. It was so obvious and cliché I mentally facepalmed at my stupidity. Minerva was a voodoo queen, with her charms in her ears and her jewelry that could have come out of a cheesy movie. If that was the case, she was also very likely the one who had made the Baron Samedi disappear. For a moment, I almost regretted not having Mom clean out the coroner's office. It likely would have saved a bunch of trouble. Godsdamned hindsight.

"You got her?" I said over my cup. Renton nodded and tossed down a fifty. We rose as one and made our way out of the café. The clouds overhead were getting heavy, making me think there would be at least a light misting. Regardless, we kept pace with Minerva, staying back about fifty feet and switching sides, though we apparently didn't need to bother as she never looked behind her. Either we were that good, which was possible, or she was that oblivious.

There was also the chance that she had already done whatever she was going to do and didn't care that she was being tailed, a distinct likelihood that I wished I hadn't considered.

After about a mile and a half of walking, I figured I needed more backup than Renton could provide. I also didn't trust using our phones because of the chance of being heard or worse misunderstood on the other end. We slowed our pace, letting Minerva get a bit farther ahead so she couldn't hear us talk. "Head back to the hotel," I said quietly to Renton. "I can follow her better alone. Once she gets where she's going, have someone come to me for backup."

"Your mother said I was to watch over you."

"One of us has to follow her. We lose her, we're likely screwed. Tonight is when the souls are released from purgatory."

"Tom, I have no knowledge of the gods other than you work for them." Renton's eyes narrowed. "Fine. Just please don't do anything rash."

"Give me a gun." When Renton balked, I looked him in the eye. "Only if I need it, okay?" He pulled out a small .38 snubnose revolver, like something out of Hawaii Five-O and handed it to me. The weapon was heavier than it had any right to be for the tiny size. I put the gun in my pants at the small of my back and dropped the tail of my shirt over it. A snubnose revolver wasn't much; but it was six more shots than I had before.

"You won't use it unless you have to?" Renton seemed almost regretful giving me the weapon.

"Scout's honor…" I paused. "You know, I don't know your first name. What is it?"

"Mister," he deadpanned. "I'll send someone once you call. I'll make sure they come here so they don't have too far to go and you don't have too long to wait." Renton did an about-face and moved swiftly out of sight, leaving me tailing possibly one of the most powerful practitioners of voodoo in the world who was leading me to where I could find out just what the hell was going on.

Oh yeah, easy-peasy lemon-squeezy.

Minerva kept going for another mile, nearly losing me in a couple of crowds and making a few sharp turns. I stayed with her, crossing a bridge with the Mississippi in view. A breeze was coming off the river, blowing back my hair and bringing the scent of the water. Another mile got us onto Peters Street after a left turn off Flood Street, warehouses springing up on both sides of the road. There were pilings of metal and stacks of metallic crates on the north side of the street on the outskirts of the warehouse area, with little slapped-together offices on blocks here and there.

As she reached a parking lot with a smattering of cars and trucks, Minerva headed straight for a huge green pickup truck, the kind with oversized mud tires and an extended bed. There were busses that were smaller, at least to my eyes. Minerva put the bags into the bed of the truck and walked for one of the small temporary buildings.

I had taken cover behind one of the huge stacks of crates and waited to see what she would do. Minerva going inside the office gave me a bit of a chance. She was getting in the truck and heading out; that seemed certain. What I needed was a way to keep up with her, and all I could think to do was the oldest and dumbest way to do it.

When I heard the truck door slam, I already knew what I was doing was both a bad and dumb idea. What was worse was I still had no clue as to where we were going. Of course, bad ideas had never stopped me before, and dumb ideas were kind of my thing. The blanket I was under hadn't moved at all, though, and I had heard her footsteps go directly to the extended cab, which led me to believe I was likely still hidden. The gun in the waistband of my pants dug into my back a bit painfully, but I gritted it out. I had more important things to worry about, such as the truck starting and beginning a bumpy ride to parts unknown.

I pulled my phone from my pocket and started one of the tracking applications I often used. The apps were useful when I needed someone to find me and I had no idea how to give directions, and when I once tossed my phone into the backseat of some lady's car to track her to where she left her husband's remains. Mac had been surprised when he got the notification, but the accompanying text had explained it well enough. That had been a fun one.

This time, though, I had thrown myself into the figurative back seat. I had a hunch that any holiday that involved releasing spirits from some kind of purgatory was worse than a murderous spouse. Let's throw in people dying across the city of New Orleans in horribly terrible ways because of the power of supposed black magic which was apparently nothing more than the stolen power of a major voodoo *loa*, who by the by was still missing. All that together added up to some kind of event that no one really wanted to happen, likely some kind of global apocalypse. This one would probably have zombies, and evil spirits trying to take some kind of twisted vengeance on the living.

I mean, we already had the cliché voodoo queen in a mud-covered hillbilly pickup, in the capital of American voodoo, the mojo bags, the mystical trappings that did little more than grab the attention of powers beyond mortal ken. Why not go the rest of the way with the dead walking around and destroying the world? It's not like it could get any worse.

Yes, I actually thought those words, but mainly because it was true. There was no possible way it could get worse.

That is, of course, when it started to sputter rain. Cussing silently to myself, I felt the water collect on the blanket and start to seep through.

I took a deep breath and let it out slowly. I hoped it wouldn't be long before Minerva got where she was going. As exposed as I was, I knew the case on my phone wouldn't keep out all the weather for long. That would put me up that famous creek *sans* paddle, a place I likely needed to start paying rent as I spent quite a bit of time there.

Peeking out from under the shoddy blanket, I watched the roofs of houses go by. For several minutes I kept count of the houses and the turns, trying to gauge just where the hell I was heading. From the intermittent sun that shone through the clouds, I figured we were heading east-northeast, which meant we were heading for the bayous if I correctly remembered the map I had read. That made things interesting, as I recalled there were several bodies found along the way to the bayous. Was it actually going to be this easy?

Houses became fewer, and the sounds of civilization became less frequent the longer she drove. We had been on the road for maybe twenty minutes at that point, and my back was turning into hamburger by then thanks to both the shitty shocks of the truck and the shoddy roads. There was no danger of my being rocked to sleep; if I got through this mess, I would have a rainbow of bruises across my back radiating from the small of my back upward. The grip of the revolver was bad enough, but the wooden stakes and other detritus pounded my shoulders and spine like baseball bats every time there was the slightest bump. I bit back a cry of pain or twenty, trying not to give myself away. Through the back window of the truck, I could see her braids atop her head. Minerva Gray seemed intent on driving, which considering the bouncing needed her utmost concentration.

After another thirty minutes or so, I heard gravel under the tires, then the splatter of mud. That went on for a minute or two before I felt the truck slow down. I almost let out a moan of relief. Wherever the hell we were, it was out in the boonies. That was both good and bad. Good because I wouldn't have to worry about bystanders getting involved. Bad because I was still without backup and would likely remain so for long enough to become a problem. I eased my hand to the small of my back and pulled out the gun, glad it wasn't a bigger automatic, as that would have likely broken my tailbone.

The wet blanket had muffled a lot of the sound, but I could hear her open and close the door, and the mud squishing under her shoes as she came around the bed of the truck. I was on the side opposite her packages, which hadn't moved that much. Listening carefully, I could only hear one set of muddy footsteps; that likely meant she was alone. Luck just might have finally been with me.

As I heard her grab the handles of the canvas bags, I threw the blanket aside, bringing a squawk from her with the water flying. I pointed the gun at her, connecting an invisible line between the barrel and her chest. "Please don't move, Dr. Gray." My voice came out as ashes from the amount of control I kept on it to keep me from ranting and screaming at her. I had too much anger for this, and it was taking everything I had to keep from just outright shooting her.

She froze, her eyes wide in surprise. "I remember you from the morgue. You're that fake doctor." She looked at me in wonder. "You're Thomas Statford. What are you doing here?"

"Trying to figure out what the hell is going on, Doctor." I saw a small shack nearby, old and rusty walls, dilapidated roof, single door and a window on each side. It looked to have been there since at least the Great Depression, and was probably as sturdy as a block house in a kindergarten class. "The better question is what are you doing here?"

"Finishing what was started." She looked at me square in the face, and there was some fear there, but not of me. Her hands slowly went up. "Doing what I must for me and mine."

I climbed down slowly, keeping the gun trained on her. "Whatever you're doing, you have to stop. You're going to stop. This is over." I could feel my anger rising again, but I put a damper on it, the rain running down my face and back helping to pull the emotion away. "We're going into that shack over there and wait for my backup. After that? Hell, I don't know, but this bullshit is over, lady. Now move it."

We walked to the ancient building, her opening the door at my command. The mud wasn't as bad the closer we got to the tiny house, so I worried more about Minerva than my footing. We walked inside to dimness, the only light being the sun slanting through the glass windows. I put the good doctor in the only chair in the one-room building, taking stock of the rest of the place. A bedframe with no mattress, a stand for a sink, metal walls that echoed with the intermittent drumming of the rain. The floor was simple wood, and creaked with each step. It was a musty little place with almost no ventilation, so I lifted up one of the windows just to get some air flowing.

"Who are you, Mr. Statford?" Minerva asked me as I leaned against one of the supports. "Why do you interfere?"

"Lady, I didn't want to interfere," I said, rolling my shoulders but keeping my gun ready. "I came down here for a vacation and to get married. I couldn't have given a damn less what you were doing. You brought me into this with a guy dying right in front of me and my future father-in-law!" I laughed humorlessly. "You wanna talk about bad first impressions? That probably takes the taco."

The look of amazement on her face was almost priceless. "You mean you weren't sent to stop the ritual?"

"I don't even know what the fucking ritual is!" I exploded. "I had absolutely no idea anything was going on! This all just fell into my lap and I've been stumbling around trying to keep my family out of it and find out what was killing these people!"

"You poor soul," she said. "You poor dear. You have no idea what you've gotten into, have you?"

I took a deep breath to bite back the bile that wanted to spew from my lips. "Lady, you are really not going to win any brownie points with me using that kind of phrasing."

"You don't know what is going on here."

"No fucking shit." Keeping an ear and an eye on Minerva, I went to the window facing out to the lonely road. "So are you going to tell me what's going on or do I have to beat it out of you?"

Minerva smiled sadly. "You are not that kind of person."

"I can learn real quick!" I snapped. A set of headlights was showing in the distance. It was either my backup or hers.

"Expecting someone?"

"Maybe. Are you?"

"When the time is right." She went still as a block of ebony after that.

The headlights approached at a pretty good clip. Either it was someone who knew the way or was really in a hurry. When I saw it was a Chevy Tahoe, I smiled. I could see the license plate was from the rental agency. Susana jumped out, a small automatic in her hand. She nearly wiped out in the mud, but caught her balance.

I opened the door and waved her inside. The rain had tapered off to nothing, but there was still lightning in the sky. I gave Susana a quick hug to welcome her. "You're my backup?"

"Would you rather my father?" She smiled back.

"No, you'll do, darlin. You'll do fine." I pointed my weapon at Minerva Gray, who still sat stock still, seemingly untroubled by our presence and the fact that her scheme was over. "This is her."

"This is who's killing those people?" Susana seemed unbelieving. "Can we get some drums or something to make it more hokey?"

"You mock what you do not understand." Minerva had let her eyes slip closed. She opened them and looked at the both of us, her gaze like a snake. "This had nothing to do with anyone outside our little group."

"Yeah, tell it to my sister's kids who are going to need years of therapy." I approached Minerva, Susana right behind me. "What were you trying to accomplish?"

Minerva let her head roll back on her neck, her braids falling free. She stood and took off her raincoat, draping it on the back of the chair. Sitting back down, she took the stance of a prim and proper doctor. Looking at her, no one would guess she was some kind of psycho voodoo priestess. I mean, she wasn't exactly wearing a sign that said it, or had "evil mastermind" tattooed on her forehead in neon ink. None of this made any sense.

"Have you ever lost someone, Mr. Statford?" She smiled again, the sadness almost heartbreaking. "Someone before their time?"

"Almost." I kept my responses to a minimum. I wasn't going to be interrogated. She was. "So?"

"What if you could bring them back from the land of the dead? That you could, by giving yourself to the *loa*, you could trade places with the one you lost?"

My response was swift. "I'd say you were nuts."

"You doubt the power of voodoo, of the *loa*."

"No, I don't doubt their power or their existence. I doubt they'd want to bring back anyone from the dead. The gods don't work like that, Doctor. Believe me, I know."

Minerva's smile grew, this time like she knew something and would tell only when she was damned good and ready. It was a bit unnerving. "The *loa* serve us, Mr. Statford, just as we serve them. One cannot be without the other."

"Knock the doubletalk bullshit off, Doctor Gray," Susana hissed. "People are dead, and it's looking like you're the one responsible."

"They all lost someone very close to them, miss. They wanted them back."

Realization hit me. "So you're killing them to bring back someone they lost? That's insane!" I looked at Minerva closely. "Did it work?"

"Not yet, but the ritual isn't over."

"What do you mean?"

"There's one more who must sacrifice themselves to complete the ritual."

"And then what? A dozen people come back from the dead like nothing happened?" Susana rolled her eyes. "That's just crazy, and you know it's not going to work."

I searched Minerva's eyes, free of deceit or trickery. "No, she thinks it's going to work. The last one is going to happen soon, isn't it?" She nodded. "Godsdammit, lady, this isn't going to work! You're just killing innocent people with their own grief."

"He's right, Doctor," Susana said. "This is crazy! You have to stop it before anyone else gets hurt."

"It is already begun." The words came out of Minerva without even a bit of sadness now. "It is how it must be."

"What about the Baron?" I said. "Why would he give you his power?"

Minerva looked surprised for a moment, then smiled broadly. "Who said I was the one who got it?"

The smile turned into a rictus of pain as blood spurted from her eyes and her hands clutched her stomach. She bent over her knees and vomited up black fluid mixed with reddish pink pieces of something. I jumped back as she fell forward, her forehead smacking the wooden floor with a horrible sound. She tried lifting herself up with one hand but couldn't find the strength. Bloody vomitus dripped from where her long braids had lain in it. Even though I had seen it twice before, I couldn't pull my gaze away. The stench from her final bowel evacuation as she died was horrid, making me gag.

I covered my mouth and tried to breathe shallowly. The open window did nothing to mitigate the smell, and I took a step towards Susana. She took my questing hand, more for mutual comfort than just for herself. I needed it, too.

"So she can't be the one," Susana said, exhaling heavily. "What the hell is wrong with this place?"

I let go of Susana's hand and stepped around Minerva's liquefying body. Putting my gun at the small of my back, my fingers gripped up her coat, a jingling coming from one pocket. I reached in and found a small mojo bag, a twin to the one I had found on at the morgue, just a lot less sticky.

I squatted down next to the body, looking down on the ruin that was once Minerva Gray. "Gods, who did this to you?" I shook my head in disgust. "Better yet, what nut convinced you to do this to yourself?"

"Tommy, it's not your fault." Susana put her hand on my shoulder. "You couldn't have known she wasn't the one."

"It fit, though." I rubbed my lips with my fingers. "Bodies show up at the morgue, Lemarchand doesn't find the bags. He doesn't find them because she gets them out before he sees them. It made sense." Laughing dryly, I said, "The only thing that actually made sense in this case. She lost someone, too, which made it even more a perfect fit."

It was about then that the answer hit me.

"Oh shit." I stood up abruptly, keeping my balance by the barest of margins. "I know who did it!"

And that, of course, was when a large heavy blunt object hit me. Lights out.

Chapter Thirteen

I hate when I'm right.

I hate it even more when I'm right when it doesn't matter.

Light came into my eyes from a pair of lanterns that had been brought in. One rested on the chair Minerva Gray had fallen from, the other on the sink stand. They were the electric kind that lit up everything in the room, and I could still see the wasted form of the dead woman lying on the floor. The stench was a bit better, and the outside was a bit darker, which meant that some time had passed since my enforced naptime.

The ropes on my wrists were tight without a bit of give, my hands behind my back. I was on my knees, being held upright by a pair of very strong hands. My ears were ringing again, this time from coming back from unconsciousness. I probably had a concussion, and I could feel blood drip in a steady flow down my neck into the collar of my shirt.

Of course, looking up at Doctor Paul Luvec, I figured a bloody shirt was the least of my worries.

Felix and Beau were there, too, looking stoned out of their minds. At least, I figured Felix was there since Beau was the one watching over Susana, holding here upright. She had a nasty gash on her arm which bled freely. Though it hurt me to do it, I looked up at who was holding me by the shoulders. Sure enough, it was my old pal Felix, staring straight ahead, slack-jawed, still wearing his work coveralls. Susana seemed conscious, but Beau had her locked down pretty well. She seemed to be bound as I was. This did not bode well.

"You couldn't leave well enough alone, could you?" Luvec's voice was still nasal, still annoying, but with an undercurrent of power I hadn't heard the last time we talked. "This had nothing to do with you, Keeper."

I hung my head. Gods, did everyone know who the hell I was on the weird side? "Doc, I didn't know what you were doing. My being here was an accident."

"Lies, but what does it matter now?" Luvec was in some kind of flowing robe, the bright colors playing off his pale skin. The glasses he wore flashed in the lantern light, and were an anachronism as his sandaled feet walked to the door. "The ritual will be complete, and no one can stop it, not even the Keeper of the Conclave."

"Look, you want to bring back a bunch of people from the dead, fine." I lifted my head to look at him. "These folks wanted to give themselves up for something stupid like that, I'm cool with it. Let me and her go and we'll let you all have your happy little reunions."

Luvec spun around, his gaze boring into me. "Is that what she told you?" When I nodded, he did the last thing I expected.

He laughed.

For a solid minute, he laughed, holding his stomach. "Oh my, that's good. That's wonderful, in fact!" When I still looked stupidly at him, Luvec calmed down. "She was right, to a point. That was originally the plan. Then I thought about it. If I have the power of the Baron, why not bring everyone back?"

Shit.

"They would be under my control, of course, but the dead would return!" Luvec sighed contentedly. "She was the one who seduced the dear Baron. Plied him with barrels of rum, crates of tobacco and her own body until even he passed out." He looked sadly at the corpse. "She gave everything for a grander plan than even she dreamed. Tonight, the breaking of the jars will be the beginning of a new age. The dead walking the earth until none living remain, and all under my control."

Double-shit. "You're trying to take over the world? Really?" I spat at his feet. "Could you twirl your mustache a little more, asshole?"

Luvec looked at the spittle, raising an eyebrow. "You have no idea what it means to lose the one who means your life, Keeper. What you would do to bring her back. What you would give up for someone else." He jerked a thumb to his chest. "I decided to bring them all back. The other wouldn't have gone along with it, so what they didn't know wouldn't hurt them."

"So you're resurrecting everyone who's ever died? That's insane. That's billions of people! What about the living?"

"What about them?" Luvec shrugged. "They will not last long. They will join the legions under my command, and peace will reign for the first time in this world. Plato once said that only the dead have no fear of war."

"And you'll be the only living thing in the world?"

"Only until I am the last. At that point, I will end my life to join the dead. It will be a fitting end to the human race. Peace through the grave."

Oh yeah, this guy was off his godsdamned rocker.

"You have no idea what it means to lose the one you love, but you will, Keeper."

"Come on, man!" I pleaded. "Let it go. Turning the world into a mass grave is not going to bring her back."

Luvec stopped and looked down on me. "No, but it will be an excellent start." He looked to Felix and Beau. "My two faithful servants. I gave you sight and knowledge. It destroyed your will, but that is of no consequence. I have a final set of commands for you both. Are you ready?"

I could see Beau nodding, and figured Felix was doing the same. Knowledge and sight my ass. Probably a mix of magic mushrooms and wormwood, along with some modern chemicals, guaranteed to keep them pliable.

"Good. I want you to wait, say, fifteen minutes. In fifteen minutes, kill her. I want him to know what it's like before he dies, so he knows what pain really is." Luvec glared at me. "I don't want to be here in case there's a backlash to killing him like he said. After she is dead, kill him."

"Okay, Doctor," Felix said. "We can do that."

"Once you're done, I want you to kill yourselves, so you can join me at the old graveyard."

"Okay, Doctor. We can do that."

"I'll be sending some help along shortly, but there shouldn't be a problem, should there?"

"No, Doctor, no problem."

"Wonderful. Time starts now. Goodbye, Felix. Goodbye, Beau."

"Goodbye, Doctor."

The door closed with the finality of a casket, and I heard an engine start up. From the sound, it was the truck that Minerva Gray had driven. That made sense, as the stuff she had picked up from the Sticks and Stones was still in the back. I was so glad things made sense now that I was likely out of chances to do anything about it.

"I'm sorry, babe," I said to Susana. "I didn't mean for you to get dragged into this."

"It's okay, Tommy." She seemed to be taking impending doom rather well.

"You know this wasn't supposed to happen. You were never supposed to get involved." I tried to slump forward, but Felix kept my back straight. I could hear him counting seconds under his breath. "We were just going to get married and be happy."

She smiled at me. "I know."

Felix was up to three-hundred-sixteen and showed no signs of stopping.

"How long was I out?" I would have given someone a thousand dollars for an icepack.

"About half an hour. Luvec was afraid that big bastard had killed you."

I couldn't see outside. "It's full dark?"

Susana nodded. "Close enough to it. No problem."

Her response floored me. There we were, about to have our necks snapped if we were lucky, and she could only say "No problem"? I heard Felix hit six-hundred-something. "Babe, you do know where we are, right?" She nodded. "'No problem'?" She nodded again.

That was when I heard the scrabbling coming from outside, the sound of bone on metal. It appeared that Luvec's help had arrived, and started getting upset as the door wouldn't open. The knob twisted and shook, but would not even move. A steady pounding began on the metal door, rhythmic and powerful. The walls of the shack shook as whatever was outside kept hitting the door like clockwork.

"'No problem'?" I smiled.

Susana shook her head. Gods, I loved that woman.

When Felix hit in the seven hundreds, I heard a pair off huge motors outside, followed by what could only be described as a cross between a rave and an inferno at a fireworks factory. There were flashes of light visible through the window, with heavier thumps against the walls of the shack. Moans and groans came from outside, cutting off suddenly when a gunshot went off, which was quite often. That went on into Felix hitting 800. When he hit 825, silence fell, with the only sounds being the counting and our breathing.

At 834, incredibly, there was a knock at the door. A light tapping, to be exact.

I looked up at Felix, who kept up the monotonous counting, then over at Beau, whose head had turned in the direction of the knock. "You might want to get that," I said. "It could be the doctor."

That lit up his face like a kid at Christmas. "The doctor?" Whatever Luvec has dosed him with had likely fried every higher brain function he had. "I should answer the door, man."

I nodded. "Yeah, you should totally do that."

Obediently, Beau made his way to the door. His hand closed on the knob and he twisted it. The door stuck at first, but swung open with a bit of muscle.

"*Buenos noches, señor,*" I heard just before a steel blade appeared out of the middle of Beau's back, growing like a metal branch. Over a foot of steel sprouted out, glistening in the lantern light. Beau made some kind of noise, a cross between a gag and a grunt, as he staggered backwards.

"Nine hundred," Felix muttered. "Time to kill the woman." He began to turn to his left but was stopped by the appearance of a knife in the right part of his chest. Another blade thumped into the left side of his chest. Another rounded out the collection in the middle. Still he stood.

Don Salvador Iglesias y Marquez walked into the shack, a knife in his hand. He threw the blade, hitting Felix in the throat. He fell backwards from the impact, landing behind me and out of my sight. Don Salvador smiled at his handiwork, then at me. "Is this a good time?"

I playfully glared at Susana. "This is why there's no problem, eh?"

"Couldn't have you feeling too safe, *gringo*."

"Thanks for the save, sir. It was getting close." Mr. Renton came in and began cutting Susana and me loose. "Thanks."

"My pleasure, Tom." Renton glanced disapprovingly at me. "My gun?"

"No match for someone coming from behind with a two-by-four."

The Don only had eyes for his daughter. "When you didn't check in, *mija*, I feared the worst." He held her close.

"It's okay, Papa. I knew where you were and I knew you were on your way."

"A very unsafe way of doing things, young lady." Mom walked in, wearing some kind of jumpsuit festooned with pockets and a web belt. "Clear, by the way. Very well done, Mister Renton."

Renton smiled and nodded his head respectfully in my mom's direction. As I rubbed my wrists to get the circulation back, he reappeared in front of me, holding out that damned revolver.

"I prefer a Beretta," I said.

"Italian trash," Renton answered. "This gun's never failed me. I want it back."

"What now?" Mom asked, bringing us back to the problem at hand.

I took the Colt, checked the loads, and put it back where I had had it before. "Luvec is trying to bring about the literal zombie apocalypse." Checking out Felix, I took one of the knives sticking out of his chest and made a makeshift scabbard out of my belt. I headed outside past Mom and the Don. Bodies were everywhere, and they were all in different states of decay. Most of them were headless, while several had neat holes in their heads. It was complete carnage.

Pushing the scene out of my head, I continued. "He's got the power to complete the ritual. He's probably waiting for midnight. Tomorrow's 'Feed The Dead' day. Supposed to be a big fun party." I went to one of the other vehicles that hadn't been there when I had arrived, a Ford pickup with a gun rack in the back. Pulling open the door of the truck released a stench of hash, burnt hair and what I could only call corruption. Holding my breath, I reached in to grab the pump-action shotguns. I put them by the truck and went in to find some shells.

"What happens at midnight?" The Don had followed me, his hands on Susana's shoulders.

"If I had to guess, Luvec finishes what he started, the dead rise, they eat the living." I began feeding ammunition into the shotguns. "It gets better. Once he's the last living thing, he kills himself. Earth becomes the undead capital of the universe."

"So where is he now?" Renton was reloading a magazine for his hand cannon.

"He said something about an old graveyard," Susana piped up. "It's probably near here, and abandoned." She looked at me. "Not likely he would be able to do something like this with a lot of people around."

I nodded in agreement. "Yeah, and dollars to donuts, that's where the Baron is."

"Thomas," Don Salvador said, "I wish you good luck, but I am taking my daughter from this." When Susana began to protest, he silenced her with a word. "I cannot lose her."

"Papa!" She pulled herself away and glared at him. "I can handle myself! You don't need to protect me from everything."

"*Mija*, you are too precious to me! I cannot allow it." He pointed at me. "Do you wish to die with this man?"

"I do."

"Babe, I have to agree with your dad," I said. "This is going to get really bad. I don't want you to get hurt."

Susana grabbed my shirt and pulled me close, kissing me. There was a heat, then a fire between our lips. I felt all my pain slipping away, filled with unending power. I put my arms around her and held her to me. When she broke the kiss, I was out of breath. She looked directly in my eyes and said "If you ever agree with my dad about something like this, I will punch you in the head as hard as I can." She smiled as she said it, but I knew she'd do it. "I love you. Today and every day from now on. We face it together."

I took a deep breath, inhaling her scent. "Yes, ma'am." I looked to the Don, who looked both proud and crestfallen. "It's pretty hard to say no to your daughter, sir."

He smirked. "So I noticed. Very well." He had his sword, a heavy blade without any real ornamentation. He sheathed it with some finality. "I will go with you."

"No, Papa!" Susana cried. "You need to take care of Mama and Paolo."

"You will also need to watch over my daughter, son-in-law and grandchildren." Mom came over to us as we had been talking. "Mr. Renton will get you back to them. I have to go with Tommy and Susana." She handed me that damned pouch, the skull grinning on it.

I shoved it in my pocket. Her statement caught me off-guard. "Why?"

"The only unused graveyard within twenty miles is near the edge of Halfmoon Pass Bay." She had a small tablet in her hand and showed the area she was talking about.

"And how do you know this?" Susana asked.

"Public records are accessible by anyone, and anyone with specific enough questions can find the answers they want." She smiled. "This was actually easy because Luvec's family was buried here before Hurricane Katrina hit. It was abandoned as being too out of the way and not of any use by the general population." Mom tapped a few commands in, and a countdown started.

"Ma, countdowns are never good." I pointed at the rapidly descending timer. "What's that for?"

"A last resort." Seeing I wasn't going to give it up, she sighed. "A thermobaric weapon will be launched at that site, destroying anything and killing anyone in the blast area."

"Gods," I muttered. "A fuel-air bomb? Really?"

"I am one of four people with the authority to perform a termination with extreme righteous prejudice on American soil." Her voice was cold. "Not even the President has that power."

"It ever occur to you that might not work?"

"Your idea?"

"We hit the graveyard and free the Baron."

Mom pursed her lips. "And if this Baron isn't there?"

I smiled. "Then we get the hell out and you TWERP it all you want."

She held back a chuckle. "You shouldn't call it that. It's very serious." Mom put the tablet away. "Very well. I'm going with the two of you. I'm the only one who can call in the strike anyway." She walked to Don Salvador and took his empty hand in both of hers. "Take care of my babies."

The Don stiffened at the request, then smiled. "It shall be done, *La Espirita*." To Renton, he said, "Come along, *señor*. We must go and protect the homefront."

Renton nodded. "Yes, sir, but we might have an issue." He raised his gun, a laser sight lighting up.

We all looked in the direction he pointed. Slumping toward us was a mass of hunched-over forms, moving slowly but inexorably. Most of them were little more than bone, but some still had flesh and muscle and clothing hanging of them. They shuffled forward, and there had to be hundreds of them. The creatures moved forward, bumping into each other, unaware of anything except the warm bodies in their path. A moan began in the crowd and was taken up by the rest.

"Fuck me," I whispered.

The Don took a deep breath and raised his blade. "Go on, Thomas. We will be fine. Won't we, Mr. Renton?"

"As soon as you get in the car, yes, we will." Renton sprinted for the Navigator he, the Don and Mom had come in.

"*Buena suerte, mija y mijo*," He embraced first Susana, then me. "Bring her home safe, son."

"Yes, sir." Tears stung my eyes.

The Navigator revved to life and Renton spun it around in the mud. Through the open window, he shouted, "Time to go, sir!"

"Us too." Mom nodded to the Don and pulled us toward the Tahoe. I slid behind the driver's seat while Susana and Mom got in the passenger seat and back, respectively. "Tommy, drive like life depends on it."

I floored the accelerator, listening to Mom call out directions. It had gotten a hell of a lot darker quicker than I thought it should, so I hit the high beams. "How far?" I asked.

"About twenty miles."

I whipped my head around to look at her before looking back at the road. "Are you serious? I thought you said it was twenty miles away!"

"As the crow flies, it's a bit over twenty-two miles. We are not crows. As mere people who can't fly, it's more like thirty-five."

Counting to ten was the toughest thing I had done, but it kept me from firing off a retort I would regret. "Okay, so I really need to hurry." I took a curve at forty, hearing the tires screech and complain as I whipped the wheel in the opposite direction in a hurry. My foot hit the gas and the speedometer went up to triple-digits.

"Tommy, we have time," Susana soothed, the shotgun she had grabbed cocked, locked and ready to rock. "Midnight, right?"

"Sure, but do you want a dramatic finish or us having absolutely no problem and no worries getting this asshole?" I took another turn, this time only twice the recommended speed. "I only say this because my mom hates dramatic finishes and will mini-nuke this son of a bitch if it looks like we won't make it."

From behind us, I heard Mom quietly say, "He's right. I will."

I think it was the calm clarity of Mom's voice that made Susana look at me, then at the road, and say, "Good idea. Go faster."

We rocketed across a bridge, getting about two feet of good air as we crossed. I maintained control by the barest of margins, the bouncing playing hell on the wound on the back of my head. The Tahoe grabbed the road again and we were moving back into high speeds. If someone had asked me where we were, the best I would have answered is "Louisiana", and the way I was driving, I would have easily allowed myself a margin of error about three states wide.

With only the headlights cutting a swath through the darkness, I felt as if I was heading back into the times past, when humans didn't venture outside when the sun went down for fear of the monsters taking them. Fog drifted in from the sides of the road, and it just added to the surrealistic landscape. Worse, the road began to deteriorate rapidly, making me slow to forty miles an hour. Still a good speed all things considered, but I didn't like going so slowly, especially with the threat of the lady behind me all too real.

"Look out!" Susana screamed.

The good news was, I saw what she was talking about before she shouted. There was a mob of the shambling things that had once been people on the road. Their backs were to us, so I saw flayed flesh and bright white bone in my headlights. The group was about eighty or ninety strong, spread over the entire road, with more pulling themselves from the ground to join the march. They were acting like they hadn't seen us yet.

The bad news was I was going too fast to brake.

Do you know what occupies most of the southeast part of Louisiana? Swamps, which are made of muddy and mostly stagnant water. It soaks in, permeating the flesh and expanding everything like a sponge. The effect on human anatomy is usually quite disgusting, especially when you careen into several of those human anatomies at fifty miles an hour. As the innards sprayed all over the windshield and I spun the steering wheel around to try and regain some semblance of control, I had time to thank whatever had made me decide to leave the windows up.

As the Tahoe shuddered to a stop, the engine made a horrid crunching noise with something like a gunshot following the initial noise. I cursed and tried the key to no response; even the starter wasn't clicking. We were in near total darkness thanks to the explosion of entrails covering the front and side windows. Believe me, blind and trapped in an non-functional vehicle was not my idea of the best position to be in while a crowd of summoned corpses were stumbling around.

Staying there was not an option, as I heard the moans from outside getting louder. I shouted for Susana and Mom to grab everything they could and get out of the car. We would do the only thing we could and make a run for it.

Mom pulled something out of her pockets that looked like a big egg. She twisted it and tossed it in the luggage area, where it started beeping contentedly. "Run!" she shouted, kicking open the door.

We followed suit, coming out in the middle of a bunch of the creatures. They had been shambling around the Tahoe; we had gotten their attention with our escape. Gods, the stench was nearly overpowering. Faces and bodies ravaged by time and the elements were surrounding me and it was all I could do to keep my sanity from telling me to fuck right off. The corruption and destruction of these people was enough to nearly make me curl up in a ball and scream until my voice broke.

My mom shouted for my attention, breaking me out of the near fugue, and tossed me a crowbar. I caught it and began to bash my way through the crowd, keeping my face somewhat covered to prevent getting any gunk on it. Fighting over to the other side of the car was a constant swinging of my arm, the metal in my hand vibrating with each successful hit. My free hand pulled out my knife, which I used to stab the creatures in the head. In most cases, my hand actually went into the skull, covering me and my weapon in disgustingly cold thick fluid.

Susana was holding her own, bashing aside those things with the shotgun. We went back to back for a moment, which allowed her to fire the weapon twice and obliterate everything in front of her in a fountain of gore. She called out for me to follow and I did, her clearing a path and me covering the rear. I heard Susana cry out from getting hit in the face and watched her crush the offender's skull with the gun butt. My weapons moved of their own accord, keeping those things from getting any closer.

Mom had gotten clear first and called us over. We made it to her after breaking through the perimeter of walking dead and tried to catch our breath. One of the things Hollywood never shows in the movies is how tiring constant combat can be, unless the fatigue is done for dramatic effect. I could have napped right then for about six months.

"There's a house over that way." Mom pointed to the north. "It's only a couple of miles down this road. We can regroup there. Let's move." She turned and began to jog up the path that thought it was a road.

Susana and I followed for several moments before being nearly bowled over by an explosion from behind. Flames engulfed everything in what looked like a hundred feet of the epicenter, which was once a Chevy Tahoe. The creatures pulling themselves out of the ground and moving our way just trundled right into the bonfire, most melting from the inferno, others becoming walking embers.

I stopped for a moment and watched how more bodies were coming out of the dirt and mud, like blasphemous crops. They shuffled and crawled after us, inexorable, unending, and constant as death. I almost couldn't move from the sheer horror of it. This was the future of the world if we failed. If Luvec went through with his ritual, what I was seeing was what would happen to everyone I loved in the world. My traitor mind sent images across my eyes, pictures in my head of Susana and my mom as walking corpses. How my sister and Arthur would appear, missing limbs and organs hanging out.

How Hannah and Jacob, their lives only just really begun, would look.

That broke my paralysis. No. Not in this or any lifetime would I allow that to happen.

We reached the house far ahead of any of the corpses and began to fortify it as best we could. Furniture, boards, whatever could be found went over the windows. It was a two-story job, old and decrepit. We just needed it to last for a bit so we could figure out what to do next. We needed a plan.

The moans coming from outside, drifting in on the wind, spoke their plans clearly.

Chapter Fourteen

I think this is where we left off.

The ground was soft, thankfully, so my botched landing didn't hurt too much. I made sure I rolled with the fall, but my bruised back and shoulders screamed in protest. Pushing myself up to a kneeling position, I saw that my arrival on the ground floor had not gone unnoticed. I scrambled to my feet, looking for the blip of light I had seen from the second story.

"Larry! Where the hell is it?" I threw the small flashbang grenade my mother had given me to buy me a little time. It went off with dazzling brilliance and the concussion knocked several of the corpses around.

Like clockwork, Larry appeared, pointing in the right direction. I began to trot that way, trying to keep a good pace. I was limping, which was a bad sign, but I was still faster than my pursuers. That was a small comfort, as I would get tired and they would likely chase me to the ends of the earth.

"Come on, Statford, move," I muttered to myself, trying to keep from falling over. The crowbar in my hand was heavy, and it took all I had not to just drop it. As it was, I knew I was probably going about this all wrong. Maybe Mom was right and her idea would work. There was very earthly little that could withstand a direct hit from a fuel-air explosive. I knew what they did, at least from reading about them. They had two explosions; the first explosive disperses the fuel, while the second ignites it. The oxygen is immediately burned up, causing a vacuum effect, pulling internal organs out through the mouth of any human unlucky enough not to be nearly vaporized by the fuel's ignition. Total and complete devastation.

The thing was, I couldn't be sure that whatever powers Luvec had stolen wouldn't protect him. Heading into the lion's den wasn't exactly a great plan either, but I was running out of both time and options. Luvec was growing stronger by the moment, with moans coming from all around me, and the sounds of the earth breaking open to release another soul like smoke from a jar.

As I hobbled, Larry would appear and point the way, letting me know of anything that might hinder my progress, be it holes in the ground or roots sticking out of the earth. Larry saw I was slowing down and tapped his wrist, where a shiny silver wristwatch hung.

"Yes, I know I'm running late," I hissed, the wrappings on my arms coming unraveled from getting caught on low-hanging branches. "I can't move any faster!"

"You must, Thomas. It is nearly midnight." Larry was implacable.

"Dammit." I pushed myself harder, finding a little bit more strength in me. "Fucking assholes have to try and kill the whole godsdamned world every time I turn around." The arm-wraps were annoying me, so I stripped them off, the dirty white cloth looking like streamers behind me. "I can't even have a godsdamned vacation without being put on a job."

"Unfortunately, those who would do harm do not have a calendar, Thomas."

Giving a look of doom to my spiritual friend, I pushed through the last of the brambles and saw the outskirts of the graveyard. Shivers went down my spine at the evident disrepair. The walls were crumbled to near-uselessness, allowing me to see several of the sepulchers in depressing detail. The above-ground tombs were worn by wind and rain, covered in black and green moss, the marble no longer white but a dingy grey where the growth was not present. An oppressive air weighed down on the site, making every breath I took seem that much more difficult. I could hear low moaning, which I had gotten used to, but also something else underneath. It was a guttural chant, words that clashed together in my head like chewed tinfoil. That had to be Luvec, finishing things up with his ritual. I had to move fast.

"Okay, Larry, since it's not really magic, any tips?" I whispered as I made my way to a nearby standing tomb, the Spanish moss sticking to my shirt as I leaned against it. Cattails growing from the cracks in the marble stuck at my legs.

"Belief fuels everything, Thomas. If he believes he can perform 'magic', then he can perform it. It is as simple as that." Larry stood close to me, mimicking my hiding.

I noticed this. "Why are you hiding? He can't see you, right?"

Larry half-smiled at me. "How do you breathers say, 'better safe than sorry'?"

Shaking my head, I conceded the point. "Belief. Right." I scuttled from one tomb to another, my feet sinking into the ground at least an inch on every step. The chant grew louder and more painful the closer I got to the source. Luvec's voice grew deeper with every word, the nasal quality of his voice gone completely. This was the voice of someone who had Power and was willing to use it because "Fuck you, I can," and that was not someone with whom to trifle.

I peeked around the last sepulcher and got an eyeball full of crazy. Luvec stood before an altar covered in blood from what might once have been a pig, the carcass discarded to the side. Torches were placed in a seeming pattern around the ritual area, with one right near me. I could see the focus of Luvec's attention was a smallish tomb, the door locked with a huge padlock, and a thick line of some white powder circling it. A pair of heavy wrought iron bars that looked like a grill was hanging by a single bolt above the door. Skulls were carved into the outside walls alongside crosses and other symbols of a type I didn't recognize.

Luvec was in full witch doctor regalia, his glasses flashing in the torchlight. His arms were raised in supplication, and the tinfoil-chewing got louder.

Pulling my gun from behind my back, I had it in my right hand and the crowbar in my left. I stepped out boldly, trying to get Luvec off-balance. I sometimes have a knack for that.

"Hey, what's up, Doc?" I shouted, training the gun on Luvec.

My words, loud and raucous, cut across the chant like a chainsaw through a piñata. Luvec stopped and looked at me incredulously. "You!"

"Me!" I smiled with a lot more confidence than I felt. "Me! Ooga-booga!" I kept the gun on him, the barrel never wavering.

"What does it take to kill you, Keeper?" His voice had regained that officious whiny tone.

"A lot more than you've got, Paulie. It's over. I'll kill you if I have to, and at this point, that's looking pretty likely." I moved toward the tomb, the smell of rum everywhere.

"Get away from there!"

"Or what? You'll work your bullshit hoodoo on me?" I laughed derisively, putting all my anger and fatigue in the sound. "Magic isn't real, you fuckhead. It never was."

Luvec screamed unintelligibly and flung his arms at me. I could see a wave of some kind of force flow from his arms toward me, dark and billowing. When it hit me, I felt it pass around me and over me like a noxious cloud. It pulled at my flesh and clothes as it moved but did nothing else other than ruffle my hair. A smile formed on my face, the first real smile in a good while. "That the best you've got? Really? I've seen ceiling fans do better."

The faux-witch doctor looked at his hands, covered in animal blood. "That was supposed to take your life and send you below," he whispered. He seemed in complete disbelief at how ineffective the attack was.

I was actually a bit shocked myself. I had played a gamble that he was using Baron Samedi's power, and I had not one, but two aces in the hole for that: my natural immunity to the powers of the gods of the Conclave, and the Baron's mojo bag in my pocket. Some would call that cheating. I call it winning. "See? Magic isn't real."

"You're going to ruin everything, you bastard!" Luvec cried, reaching into his robe and pulling out a knife, the silver blade shimmering in the torchlight. "I was supposed to bring peace to the world!" He glared at me. "And you will not stop me! Get him!"

That's what I got for not paying attention. A half-dozen corpses pulled themselves from the shadowy perimeter and lunged at me. I felt their scabrous claws on my arms and tearing the shirt from my back. I kicked out at one, driving its knee backwards. I followed up with a stab through the forehead with the forked end of the crowbar. Stepping out of the way, I pulled the tool out from where I had plunged it, twirled it in my hand, and swung it in a long arc at another head. It connected solidly, the impact barely noticeable from the amount of adrenaline I had going through my system. I backed away toward the center of the circle, trying to keep the remaining four in sight.

I felt my pocket grow warm as I approached the tomb, and the aroma of rum got stronger. There was a subsonic hum that rattled my fillings, making me wince. It almost sounded like singing mixed in with half-stifled laughter. I almost smacked myself in the head with my crowbar. Where else would you hold a *loa* of life and death?

The four corpses attacked simultaneously, making me stumble and flail wildly. I stopped my fall just before my head smacked into a raised piece of marble. One of the critters grabbed my shoulder, trying to pull me away. I felt the sharp bones break skin and blood started to flow down my back. I shoved myself to the left and fired my gun. Four times it barked, and four bullets found their way into their skulls. The backs of their heads exploded and the creatures dropped like puppets with their strings cut.

I turned away from Luvec, who had begun screaming incoherently, and put the crowbar's hook end between the hasp and the marble door. I put it in from the bottom so I could put my entire weight on the bar if needed. Looking down, I saw I had scuffed the white line into uselessness, and there was an eerie light coming from the underside of the door that hadn't been there when I had started to pry the lock off the door. I gave it an experimental pull down and felt a touch of give, and the door began to vibrate.

"Arise, my family!" Luvec screamed, his voice cracking. "Stop him!"

That's about when all hell broke loose.

Marble flecks flew everywhere as tombs exploded open around me, disgorging ancient dry skeletons and partly rotted bodies still wearing what was left of their Sunday finest. Sunken cheeks, empty eye sockets, open mouths with maggots dripping out, Luvec's family came for me. They were fast, very damned fast and grabbed at me as I jumped out of the way. I rolled onto my side, watching one of Luvec's relatives impale himself on the crowbar I had left. It moaned a bit then just stopped trying to free itself, as if it realized the futility.

I wasn't so lucky with the rest of the Luvec clan as I took a hit to the back of the head from one, then a vicious claw across my chest, bringing more of my blood out. A cry of pain escaped me; I couldn't help it. I had nothing left, I was out-numbered, and there was no way in hell I was going to make it back to that crowbar.

"Bring him to me! I want his blood on my knife!" Luvec squealed. Claws closed on me, gripping my wrists and arms. I was held immobile, and a hand gripped me by my hair, pulling my head up and exposing my throat. It was Luvec himself, and there was pure madness and murder in his eyes. "You nearly did it, Statford. You nearly ruined everything. I will need to infuse the barrier with the soul of a human, so it might as well be yours. You die today, Keeper." He brought the knife down in an overhand strike.

I did the only thing I could do: I slumped, just let all the strength go out of my legs. I'm not exactly a lightweight, so the sudden dead weight pulled me out of the way and pulled the rotting corpse of an old woman into the path of Luvec's blade. It buried to the hilt in her skull, dropping her instantly. Luvec let off a high-pitched cry of "Nana!" and even though he was an evil bastard and she was dead, I still felt a tiny bit bad for using her as a shield.

Not a lot, but a little.

I scrambled through the mass of arms and bones and made it in the clear. Luvec was crying as he began wrenching the blade from his Nana's head, but saw me point the gun at him. I smiled. "Looks like you're in trouble. This is a .38 snub nosed revolver, one of the most over-used piece of shit guns in the United States and some of Canada. Hell, maybe even Mexico. It fires a bullet just like every other gun out there, just really badly. It carries six bullets at a time." I got a squint in my eye and growl in my voice. "Now, in all the excitement, I forgot just how many I fired. Could be five, could be six." I thumbed back the hammer. "I don't think today's your lucky day."

"Killing me won't stop things, Keeper," Luvec snarled, finally working his knife free. "Without someone to control the dead, they will still rise at the stroke of midnight, and they will destroy everything in their path. Who else can do it? Certainly not you!"

The smug look on his face made me want to pull the trigger anyway. I could have done it. This little wiggler wanted to kill the entire world just to make sure no one else could die. That ranked up there as one of the most self-deluded things I had ever heard, and I'd heard quite a few in my years of being the Keeper. Demons starting Armageddon, someone trying to become a god, a few others, but this was way the hell up there.

However, he was probably right. If Luvec died, there wouldn't be any check on the dead rising. It would be simply a matter of attrition, and not all the fuel-air bombs in the world would stop it. That left me with only one option.

"So, Doc," I smiled broadly. "Want to see a magic trick?"

Luvec eyed me warily. "I thought you didn't believe in magic."

"I learned it a long time ago. Comes from a story I read about Sir Isaac Newton, with a little Archimedes mixed in." I raised my gun again and aimed. Not at Luvec, though. That would have been a waste of a bullet.

I fired at the bolt above the door. The grill, at least two hundred pounds or so of solid iron, crushed the corpse under it and caught on the crowbar, still jutting from under the hasp. The lock fell to the ground after the grill landed with a horrendous crash. Mud and shards of marble flew everywhere, making me cover my eyes.

I uncovered and smiled at the only other living soul in a couple of miles. "Eureka, motherfucker."

The door of the sepulcher flew out across the graveyard, shattering against Luvec's altar. There was a complete inky blackness in the tomb, not allowing me to see in. A right leg stepped out, bare, dark-skinned and muscular, with a fanciful tattoo of leg bones on it. A left hand gripped the side of the door, slowly and purposefully. Similar bones were tattooed on it. Out of the black came a booming laughter, followed by the rest of the Baron Samedi. He was a tall, well-built man, showing off his physique by wearing simply a loincloth, a silver necklace and a bowler hat. All over his brown skin were drawings of bones that looked like what a child would consider bones. What I had taken for tattoos were actually just his skin. He walked barefoot over the ground, not seeming to notice the sharp marble.

He reached Luvec, who was gibbering a mixture of the Lord's Prayer, three different psalms, and a popular children's song. The

Baron grabbed Luvec by the throat and pulled him close. "Oh, have I many things to teach you, little man. You are mine." With that said, the Baron kissed him, breathing the doctor's soul out of his mouth. When nothing but a husk of the man remained, the *loa* tossed the body aside, where it shattered into dusty remnants. The Baron then turned his glowing eyes on me.

I lowered my gun, totally empty now, and nodded to the newly-released *loa*. "Baron." My voice was a little unsteady, though considering I didn't think I would still be alive, I would allow myself the moment of vocal weakness.

"Keeper!" The Baron seemed none the worse for wear from his captivity. "So good to finally meet you, though I wish it was under better circumstances!" The voice was booming and jovial, though a bit scraggly which likely came from the copious amounts of rum he drank and the insane amounts of tobacco he chewed. "I believe you have something of mine?"

I reached into my pocket and tossed him the mojo bag. "We good?"

He caught it in midair and held it to his nose, taking a deep breath of the leather. "Ah, I have missed this. You don't know what you are missing until it is gone, yeah?"

"Glad to help, Baron. I'll be heading out now." I began to walk back the way I came into this charnel graveyard.

The Baron Samedi held up a finger, catching my attention. "You have freed me. You have returned my power to me. I owe you a boon, and the longer the wait, the greater the weight."

"I'm good. Really."

"I do not like owing mortals, Keeper. It is unseemly." Though nearly naked and wearing that ridiculous hat, there was an imperiousness about him.

"I'm not just any mortal, and since you're pushing the issue, we'll just save it for when I'm not tired and shagged out and ready to fall the hell over. Now, if you'll excuse me." I stopped. "And before I forget, you might want to make all these dead folks that are walking around go back where they came. It might do bad things to the tourism around here."

A rousing laugh came from behind me as I walked away. "You are just as they said, Keeper!" The Baron shouted after me. "You are just absolutely the best! Thank you! It will be a pleasure owing a favor to you!"

Just what I needed: a rum-swilling, tobacco-chewing, skirt-chasing *loa* wanting to do me favors. Just peachy.

I put it out of my mind as I made the trudge back to the house Susana and my mom were holed up. I took my time, not completely by choice as my legs were aching and cramping and I was bleeding from just about every bit of exposed skin. True to his word, the Baron had sent the souls back to the underworld, and returned their shells to their components, which in most cases was mud and dust. The sight of so many human-shaped piles of mud was disturbing, but only because I knew what they once were.

By the time I got to the house, I had been walking at least an hour. Outside the house was the Lincoln and another truck, this one looking like a park ranger's all-terrain type vehicle. Renton was there, helping Mom and Susana to the Navigator. The Don was there as well, holding court with a hapless park ranger who was starting to figure out just how out-classed he was.

"Mr. Marquez, this is protected land, and someone obviously blew up a car in this land," the ranger said. "If it wasn't them, then who was it?"

"Sir," the Don exuded a subtle mix of charm and menace, "I will happily take care of any damages incurred in this terrible accident."

"Accident? A car blew up!"

"Yes, an accident, *señor*." Don Salvador drew himself to his full height and looked down on the ranger, who suddenly seemed unsure of himself.

Susana saw me and shrugged off Renton's hand. A flicker of annoyance went across Renton's face until he saw who she was running for, and the annoyance was replaced by a look of pleasure.

Susana ran to me and jumped into my arms, kissing my face all over. I returned the affection, the both of us trying to devour each other with kisses. We held each other after that, just feeling the presence of the other and loving every second.

I broke away first, tears standing in my eyes, while she was openly weeping. I pulled the ring she had given me off my pinky finger. The stone was still there and shone through the mud and grime. "I think this belongs to you." She reached for it and I pulled away. The puzzlement in her face left in a flood of happy tears as I knelt before her again. "I'm gonna ask again, darlin, just to make sure you know what you're getting into. Will you marry me?"

She nodded so enthusiastically I thought her head was going to come off. "Yes!" she cried, letting me slip the ring on her finger. Susana dropped to her knees and embraced me, her breath hot on my neck, tears wetting my skin.

We stayed like that for a while, and it was good.

Epilogue

The silver wedding ring was a welcome weight on my finger as I walked into the Fly By Day travel agency. Susana and I had relaxed quite a bit afterward, but we made sure that the wedding was on the first of May. Once she knew what April 30th was for the voodoo set, she demurred.

It was a nice wedding, if you're into that sort of thing. I had the easy job, as I was told repeatedly by my mother. All I had to do was answer the question correctly, while Susana had the more difficult job of putting on a gown, walking down the aisle, answering the question and dealing with me for the rest of our lives.

Abuse, folks. Some people have to pay for it, yet I get it for free. How lucky can one guy be?

I walked to the desk where I had first made the acquaintance of Aletha Dallas. Unsurprisingly, she wasn't there. Instead, there was a rather dull man named Howard Schmertz, who could pass for the exact opposite of The Most Interesting Man in the World. I sat down in front of him as he seemed to, rather unsuccessfully, talk someone into actually going to Wyoming of their own free will. As he hung his head and hung up the phone in defeat, he noticed me for the first time.

"May I help you, sir? Interested in a trip to Wyoming?" He asked me hopefully.

I shook my head. "Actually, I was wondering what happened to Aletha Dallas. She booked a trip for me and I wanted to thank her for such a wonderful time." Said thanks was a fistful wrapped around a roll of quarters in her likely god-like skull, but that didn't need to be known at that point, especially by this probably mere mortal.

"Dallas, you said? We don't have one by that name," he said. He looked through an old-fashioned Rolodex, searching for the name I had given him.

"She was fired? She quit?"

"Actually, we've never had anyone by that name work here, sir. I'm sorry."

My shocked face must have shown. Oddly enough, it looks a lot like a pure neutral expression. "Really? Is that so."

"I've been here fifteen years and I've never heard that name. When did you come in?"

"It was last November, if my memory serves."

"Then it couldn't have been here. We were closed for renovations the entire month. Newer equipment and everything."

"I see." I was seething inside. I should have known.

"I'm terribly sorry, sir. Perhaps you'd like a brochure, in case you want to take another trip to get away from it all?"

I stood abruptly. "No thanks. I think I'll be able to get away from it all right here." I stalked out of the agency, likely leaving poor Howard sitting there, shocked, his mouth open.

Steadying my hand to open the Black Beauty's door, I got inside my car and sat. After a moment, I said, "Larry."

Instantly, he was there, seated in the passenger side. "What is it, Thomas?"

"Aletha Dallas. Who is she?"

"Aletha was the goddess of truth, similar to Apollo. There is no god called Dallas," Larry said, then paused as he searched his memory. "There is someone called Dolos, a spirit of trickery and deceit. I am sorry, Thomas. If I had known, I would have said."

My hands squeezed the wheel so tightly my knuckles went white. "I know. That's why I'm telling you first. I quit."

Larry did a double-take. "You what?"

I twisted the key savagely, the engine coming to life. "I'm done, Larry. I nearly lost my entire family down there. I almost lost Susana because some fucking god lost his handbag!" Had anyone been in the parking lot, they would have thought a crazy man was screaming at himself. "You think I give a shit about them anymore, when they obviously don't give a shit about me? Fuck em! I'm out. Tell them to find another sucker.

"I quit."

Well, that was unexpected. I don't think we're done with the Chronicles quite yet, though. Be ready for the next volume of the Statford Chronicles: All Good Things. See you then, and thanks for reading. This isn't over.

www.ingramcontent.com/pod-product-compliance
Lightning Source LLC
Chambersburg PA
CBHW070822120626
46556CB00002B/619